Dragonfly Wishes

A Fairy Tale Retelling

Rochelle K. Bradley

DEDICATION

For Hadley

ACKNOWLEDGMENTS

For my beta readers: Brandy, Laura, Scars, and Jessica. Thank you for helping me perfect Dragonfly Wishes. You rock!

To authors Andi Lawrencovna and Kali Willows: Thank you for encouraging me to find my inner dragon shifter and for all those late night talks *coughs* writing sessions. I get a charge out of you and appreciate your friendship.

PROLOGUE

MY GOVERNESS, ELYSE, discovered the portal high in a tree and swore me and my brothers to secrecy. "A gateway to another world," she'd called it. The view had looked much like our kingdom, with towering trees and a grassy meadow sprinkled with yellow buttercups, but the silver dragons never flapped their wings, and instead of breathing fire, they left smoke trails.

The small shimmering portal smelled of magic, but since it was high in a crook of a tree trunk, it remained unnoticed by most. Fascinated with the view, I visited the forest daily and climbed the tree. My brothers knew my routine, but only one suspected my true interest. *Arianna*.

A shadow passed overhead, and I glanced through the branches. My nails dug into the bark as a gust of wind tried to unseat me. The wings of a black dragon kept the beast aloft, hovering.

"I found you, little brother," the dragon's voice rumbled. With only the sound of the leaves rustling, the wings beat faster as it lowered its hulk to the mossy forest floor.

I glanced at the golden-haired woman on the other side of the portal window, then let go of the branch and jumped to the ground.

1

"I wasn't hiding," I said with a frown. "Why are you here, Jett?"

A tendril of smoke rose from Jett's nostrils. He arched his long neck and flexed his claws. As he closed his eyes, he shifted from a massive black dragon to a man of average size. Nude, he spread his arms. "I've come because our mother desires to speak with you."

"Is it about the ball?" I asked, staring up at the cloudless sky.

Jett tilted his head, his gaze sizing me up. "Yes. You are to be fitted for new attire."

I grunted.

"Kyan, our mother is the queen. She and Father only want what is best for you." Jett placed his large hand on my shoulder.

"If you say so," I muttered.

The Harvest Moon dance was held the same time each year. A chance for nobility to mingle, but also a place to find our mates. My brothers and sisters eagerly anticipated the event and I enjoyed visiting with my extended family, but...

"How is she today?" Jett asked, shifting his glance toward the portal.

"Arianna cries." I crossed my arms. "And I long to comfort her."

"But, Kyan, entering that world is risky." Jett shook his head.

"Life is risk." I smirked, and he slugged my arm. "If I go, I will take heed. It's possible she has returned to the shop by now."

"Is the uncle causing her angst again?" Jett asked as he leaned against the tree trunk.

"Her face is marred as if she's been hit." I turned away, balling my fists. The orphaned girl had grown up under the care of a ruthless tyrant. He worked her at home and the store, barely paying her. The dark circles under her bright eyes were usually there, but she still smiled.

The time in the woods gave her peace and energized her. She'd bring a pencil and draw. I loved when she sketched. Her forehead crinkled as she concentrated. Creating was her outlet, and I revered watching her escape.

"I'm sorry, Kyan." Jett's warm hand weighed on my shoulder again. "I know you care for the girl, but what can you do?"

"I heal her hands." Staring defiantly at Jett, I dared him to retort.

"Why? What's wrong with her hands?" he asked.

I relaxed my arms and lifted my fingers, wiggling them. "She designs clothing for entertainment. The tools of her trade wound her."

"Bleeding on the cloth can't be normal," Jett said with a puzzled expression.

"No, brother. She hides her work from her uncle, working in the night hours with dim light." I thought Arianna was talented. The fashions were odd but the quality solid, at least from what I could see.

"Ah," Jett nodded. "I'm glad you can do this for her. Does she realize what you do?"

I shook my head. When I maneuvered through the portal I shifted, not into my dragon form, but into a dragonfly. Being tossed about by the wind and watching out for predators had been an unfamiliar experience.

The first time I entered her world, I had hovered near her prone body. When she glanced up, she had wiped the tears away and smiled. "Hello there," she had greeted. She'd stretched out her hand and I floated over, landing on her finger.

Ever since that initial visit, when she saw me, she called me friend.

"I'm careful." I nodded to my older brother. "She does not know what I am or where I come from."

"It's a shame she doesn't follow you home," Jett said, walking toward the clearing. He stretched his arms out, then

3

shifted. With his wings tucked to his side, he arched his neck so his amber eyes gazed into mine. "Come fly with me," his deep voice rumbled.

"How about this evening?" I replied as he unfurled his wings. Jett nodded his colossal head and lifted into the air.

As soon as my brother was out of sight, I climbed the tree and settled into my spot, gazing once more through the hole at the lady in another world. Arianna had dried her eyes and opened her ever-present sketchbook, once more escaping to into her own altered reality. As a smile replaced her grave expression, my heart raced, surveying her classical elegance. The line of her jaw, her small upturned nose, and sensitive silver-gray eyes all appealed to me and my dragon.

My dragon wanted to fly to her and protect her, but as a dragonfly I wasn't sure I could.

CHAPTER ONE

ARIANNA TRAVERS SAT eyes closed with her back against her favorite tree.

"He won't break me," she mumbled. Her eyes popped open, and she swiped the tears away.

She opened her backpack and removed a sketchbook and charcoal pencils. Flipping through the pages, she settled on one with a woman wearing a shirt with wide diagonal stripes and a collar.

Arianna studied the design, then added more shadow. She pulled back the book, examining the style once more. "Better."

She set the pad aside and reached into her backpack again. Her fingers caressed soft cloth. During the dark of night, Arianna had stitched together the blouse in secret, making it from scraps she'd recycled from her uncle's store. The shirt had been her brainchild, but her uncle would yell at her if he knew she'd used the material, even though she'd found it in the trash.

Tears threatened to return, but she blinked them away. Glancing at the time, she stretched with a sigh.

Fluffy clouds floated silently overhead. The leaves fluttered with the touch of the breeze. "I wish I could leave here," she told the forest.

The screech of metal hinges echoed through the glen.

Arianna rushed to stow her art supplies.

"Where is that girl? Arianna, you lazy mooch, get your act together and get to work! I don't pay you to frolic with woodland creatures," a gruff voice hollered.

Arianna peeked around the tree, watching the back door to her uncle's store. Her uncle, Ansen Floyd, glared in the opposite direction, then returned inside.

Arianna's shift didn't begin for another half an hour, but that hadn't kept her uncle from harassing her. She sighed and rose, dusting off her rear. She slung her backpack over her shoulder.

"Help," a light, high-pitched voice called.

Arianna glanced around, searching for a child.

"Over here," it said again.

She moved closer to the broad tree across from her. "Where are you?"

"Look up. Please hurry."

A spiderweb strand shimmered in the sunlight. She followed the illuminated silk toward the tree trunk.

A blue dragonfly struggled on the web. "My little friend, what has happened to you?" His movements had caught the attention of a hairy brown spider.

"Will you help me?" the dragonfly pleaded.

"I'm going insane." Arianna rubbed her eyes.

"No, you are not." He wiggled his legs, vibrating the web. "I'm Kyan. Please, save me, Arianna, and I will grant your wishes."

"I—" she started. "Sure, I'll get you out of there." She reached up, but the dragonfly was just out of her reach. "Wait."

"Waiting is all I can do," he said, "but the spider won't."

Arianna fished in her backpack, retrieving a pencil. Holding the point in her fingers, she lifted the pencil toward the web. The eraser penetrated the silk, sending the spider scuttling toward the tree trunk. Strands floated on the wind.

Arianna angled the eraser under the dragonfly. His tiny

feet gripped it. Slowly, she pulled the pencil downward, avoiding the web.

She examined the dragonfly. His wings had tangled in the sticky spider silk. He tried to stretch, but the strands held.

"Careful, it'll rip your wing," she cautioned. "I can get it off, but I need better lighting and my magic eye."

"Magic?" Kyan canted his head.

She shook her head. "It's a magnifying glass I use for delicate needlework."

"Hmm."

"Arianna." This time a woman's voice floated over the wind. Arianna glanced around the tree toward the business. Her coworker stood with hands on her hips. "You should hurry while the Evil Overlord is in his office on a call with the bank."

"Overlord," the dragonfly grumbled with a deeper tone.

"Your belly is glowing yellow." She lifted the pencil for a better look.

"It's nothing," Kyan said, rubbing a set of his legs over his side.

"Casey refers to my uncle Floyd as the Evil Overlord. He owns the silkscreen business and boutique, but without Casey and I he'd be lost." She hitched her backpack. "I need to go. My supplies are in the shop. Are you okay with going inside or would you prefer to stay out here?"

"There are spiders out here…" His wings vibrated.

"And you can't fly. Very well, you're coming with me." Arianna nodded, pressing her lips together. Cupping the pencil top like she would protect a candle flame, she hustled toward the store.

"What do you have there?" Casey asked, studying Arianna's hands.

Glancing at the talking bug, she smiled. "A friend who needs a little help. Isn't he a beautiful shade of blue?"

"How do you know it's a he?" Casey's brow crinkled as a wicked grin spread over her shiny red lips. "I recognize that tone. You've been inspired." She opened the back door and held it while Arianna walked inside.

"Maybe," Arianna glanced at the dragonfly. "I need to fix this little guy's wings first."

Arianna placed Kyan on her workspace and slung her backpack on the chair. "I'll be back in a few minutes."

He nodded. "I'm not going anywhere."

Arianna clocked in and made a show of straightening so Floyd wouldn't gripe.

When her uncle retreated into his office again, Casey whistled, and Ariana slipped into the backroom. She found her monocular magnifier in her desk drawer. Plopping into her chair, she noticed Kyan sitting with his front legs crossed.

"Are you ready?" she asked, leaning over the desktop.

Kyan stood, tilting his head. "Yes."

"Okay. Turn around." Taking the smallest needle, she worked on removing the strands one by one without damaging the delicate skin of his transparent wings.

"Done." Arianna dabbed her dewy forehead. "Phew. How do you feel, Kyan?"

He fluttered his wings and lifted off the table, then settled down a moment later. "Perfect. Thank you for saving me from a certain demise. Let me grant your wish."

Arianna tucked a strand of her long blond hair behind her ear. She shook her head. "I wouldn't know what to wish for."

CHAPTER TWO

"ARIANNA!" THE OVERLORD hollered. "Where is that girl?"

Arianna rolled her eyes and pushed up from the chair. "I'll be back," she mumbled to Kyan, scurrying in the direction of the demanding voice.

Floyd pointed the remote toward the wall mounted flat screen. Regardless of Arianna's reminding him the store wasn't a sports bar, the local channel blared.

Sunlight streamed through the dusty front windows and glass door. The entry mats needed a vacuum.

Floyd's tie slanted to the right, like he'd been leaning when he put it on. He ran his fingers through the remaining hairs of his comb-over.

"Yes?" Arianna approached him near the TV.

His gaze darted her way, meeting hers with a scowl, then flew to the screen when a commercial for an automobile dealer began playing. The jingle echoed in Arianna's mind as it played on-screen.

"Turn your gloom into a zoom. Never assume dire doom. At Smiley Pete's showroom, get a new car and go vroom," the sickly sweet voice singsonged. A pretty redhead woman, local celebrity, Eva Adams, motioned to the cars with an inviting grin. "Come to Pete's and let him make you smile too," she cooed.

Floyd loved when the TV showcased Eva. He'd met her at a mall when she'd modeled for a charity event, and he boasted how someday he'd get her to advertise for him. Although she'd never looked twice at any offer he had sent her.

After the commercial ended, Floyd turned to Arianna. "What were you doing?"

"Talking to a dragonfly," Arianna replied. Floyd's brows dipped together, forming a V, and his face reddened. She continued, "And he told me he'd grant me a wish."

With his hands on his thick hips, Floyd huffed, "You had better hope Eva Adams walks through that door."

"You wish." Arianna couldn't help rolling her eyes.

Floyd leaned in. "Yes, I do. Why don't you ask your magic bug for that? What's in your hair?"

Something tickled her scalp, and Arianna's hand flew to the top of her head. Wings quivered at her touch. "It's my…" She paused, glancing at the TV. "It's my barrette. Do you like it?"

Floyd squinted, wrinkling his nose. "Ah, the magic bug. Hilarious." He pointed to the T-stand nearest him. "These racks need dusted."

Arianna sighed. "I'll get right on it."

The door opened, and a customer entered. Floyd grinned his tomcat-spots-a-canary smile, ignoring Arianna, as he approached the man. "How can we help you today, sir?"

Arianna hurried toward the checkout desk and retrieved the large rainbow static dusting wand. She worked her way around the sales floor, hitting the tops and bottoms of each rack. The three local schools had racks of apparel near the door. Most of their customers were parents or grandparents of the students wanting the perfect school-spirit gift.

She hadn't been able to talk her uncle into using any of her designs for novelty tees until a teenager and her mother visited the store one fateful afternoon. They began discussing the girl's college ambitions, which included designing clothing. Her mother gushed about the daughter's ability, and soon the teen and Arianna were sharing their sketches.

Arianna attempted to rub the pang in her chest away, remembering the bittersweet way she'd longed for her missing mother. She smiled at the teen's good fortune, being able to follow her dream and attend college, but more importantly having doting parents.

When the teen's mother had praised her uncle, he reluctantly picked one of Arianna's drawings to feature. The first ten shirts flew off the rack. He unceremoniously agreed she could design a shirt of the week. At first, they hung at the front of the store, but now they'd been moved toward the rear, near the fitting room.

"I know that expression," Casey whispered. "Your thoughts are in the clouds. You're planning a new design. Well, go to it. Hurry before the Evil Overlord gets free."

Arianna pressed her lips together and nodded. "I'll be quick. I know exactly what I want to do."

"You go, girl," Casey said, fist bumping her.

With one last glance toward her uncle, Arianna hurried into the backroom. She opened the sketchbook, flipping until she came across a sketch of a dragonfly. Its abdomen pointed downward while the wings formed a wide X. Arianna snapped a picture of the drawing and added it to her design portfolio. She pulled out her laptop and started the fashion program.

"Is that me?" Kyan asked, landing next to the sketch.

"It could be, if you're the only blue dragonfly," she answered with a smirk. She traced the drawing into the program, adding blue, indigo and purple.

"I've watched you draw many times," he said, fluttering onto the keyboard's 2 key. "Your art is divine."

Arianna chuckled, shaking her head. She had no family complementing her, yet she was encouraged by an insect. "Thank you. I hope to make people happy."

"In my realm, your work would be legendary." He rose,

hovering when she hit the print key.

"Maybe I could visit your world someday."

"I'd like that." Kyan floated at eye level.

"But for now I'm just a wannabe." Arianna glanced at her shoes before retreating to the printer.

Delighted with the final design, she signaled Casey, who brought her a stack of shirts. The mottled cobalt blue was lovely, but it was too dark for the colors she'd chosen. "What's with this blue?" Arianna asked.

"The Evil Overload deemed it worthy of your art," she announced with a slight sneer.

"Meaning it wasn't selling and it wouldn't hurt to give me a shot," Arianna said.

"Bingo."

"It's a pretty color. I think we have some of that iridescent ink left. It would look great on this deeper hue." Arianna took a shirt, laying it on the press as she waited for it to heat.

Thunder boomed, the lights flickered, and then rain let loose, beating the roof.

"Geez, I hope the power doesn't go out. It would be impossible to work in the dark, and the Overload won't let us leave. Remember when the transformer blew?"

"Don't remind me." Arianna pulled the handle, pressing the design to the fabric. The first was always a surprise. Her creation, her baby. She took her time squaring each design.

"I'll check the weather and see if the radar is on the screen." Casey stalked into the front of the store, leaving Arianna to her thoughts.

When she released the press and raised the fabric, glancing at the lines, it was perfect.

"Oh no!" Casey cried.

Arianna ran into the store. She tossed her new creation on the counter and dashed to the window next to Casey and Floyd. In the pelting rain, a large SUV with an obvious flat tire had pulled off the road and into the parking lot.

A woman opened the vehicle's door and slid out, holding a

substantial handbag over her head. Her lips moved, but Arianna couldn't see a phone.

"That's not very ladylike," Floyd chuckled.

"How do you know what she's saying?" Casey asked.

Floyd snickered again. "Just read her lips. Some words are universal."

The woman kicked the flat tire, then stomped toward the store.

"Oh no. She's really angry." Casey chewed her lip.

"Poor thing." Arianna opened the door for the woman. "Are you all right?"

"Thanks. Nothing a stiff drink, dry clothes, and a trip to the Keys wouldn't fix." She dropped her wet bag, then wiped her face.

Casey brought a roll of paper towels.

"Thank you. Oh crap, I left my phone in the car."

"You can use ours," Floyd said.

"I need to call roadside assistance." She took the handset and dialed. "Hi, this is Eva Adams. My piece of junk car popped its tire. I don't know the address. Hold on." She cupped the receiver and peered up at Floyd.

With his chin to his chest and his eyes bugging out, Floyd stammered, "Uh… uh."

Eva Adams? Arianna glanced around, finding Kyan sitting on her latest creation, his little legs crossed. She swore his belly glowed again.

CHAPTER THREE

CASEY HANDED EVA a business card with the address and phone number. After she hung up, Floyd found his tongue.

"Oh, Ms. Adams," he said, smiling and running his fingers through his wispy hair. "Please, if you want to get out of your wet clothes, you're welcome to pick anything in the store to wear. It's on the house."

Eva nodded and turned around, inspecting the apparel. Her eye caught the pile of blue fabric on the counter. She picked it up. It unfolded, and Kyan flew away.

"Oh my, this is marvelous," she said.

"That's one of Arianna's designs. She just made it." Casey eagerly pointed to Arianna.

Eva met her gaze. "It's gorgeous."

Arianna's face heated. "Thank you."

"I think I'll try it on." Eva glanced around the store.

"The fitting room is this way, Ms. Adams." Floyd pushed past Casey, leading the wet woman away from his employees. He hovered near the fitting room, waiting.

Casey grabbed Arianna's arm and pulled her to the backroom. "Girl, you need to make more of those shirts right now."

"Okay, but…" Arianna stared after Casey when she pranced out of the room. Arianna shrugged and started making the rest of the blue shirts. Casey would return every so often and hang the dragonfly T-shirts, then take them to the sales floor.

On the last blue shirt, Floyd approached her wearing a smile. "I can't believe Eva Adams is here. In my store. What luck."

"It's a wish come true," Arianna said wryly.

Floyd's faced reddened. "She's a classy lady. I just wish she'd advertise our store. We would get new business for sure. Everyone in town loves her."

Casey appeared next to Floyd. "You'll have to make more of those shirts in all colors and maybe long-sleeved too. I heard Eva say she'd like to buy her niece a hoodie." She touched Floyd's arm. "Eva's help is here and so is a news crew."

"What?" Floyd jumped and ran through the backroom to the store.

Casey laughed, watching him go. "You know I had to take a picture of your uncle and Eva Adams. He wanted one to frame and hang on the wall. I got one with just her where you could see your design. I sent it to you."

"Thanks. Is there really a news crew out there?" Arianna hung the last shirt and handed it to Casey.

"Yep. A big van with the dish thingy on top and everything. The rain has stopped and the sun is shining. I wouldn't be surprised if there's a freaking rainbow in the sky." Casey sashayed onto the sales floor with Arianna following.

Outside, Floyd stood next to Eva as a reporter interviewed her. She pointed to her tire, then threw her hands up. She grinned and tugged her shirt.

Arianna smiled at the recognition her design received. A fountain of joy bubbled up, and she giggled.

The repairman called Eva away and left her uncle with the reporter. With the red tipped microphone in his face, he puffed out his chest. He conversed with the reporter for a while, nodding and exposing more teeth than Arianna knew he had.

"Look. Look!" Casey pointed.

Arianna whirled around and stared at the TV. The interview was playing live. Casey turned up the volume, and they listened to Floyd claim the rescue of Eva Adams. The reporter moved toward the vehicle, and the cameraman focused on the ruined tire.

"Eva Adams was very lucky indeed when her tire blew and she hit a flooded pothole during a deluge. Shaken by the incident, she found her nerve and made her way to a local business. Floyd's Apparel and Embroidery welcomed her with open arms and dry clothes," the reporter said. The camera panned the front of the beige strip mall, then focused on the signage over the door.

"Charlie," Eva called to the reporter.

"Yes, Ms. Adams." The cameraman zoomed in on the lovely actress.

"At Ansen Floyd's store, get new clothes others will adore," she sang.

"Holy cow! She made a jingle for the store," Casey said. "I'll grab the vacuum. I bet we are going to see a crowd." Arianna agreed with a nod but kept her eyes glued to the screen. Eva had advertised the business like her uncle had wished. Arianna swallowed and rubbed her stomach.

CHAPTER FOUR

ARIANNA SLOUCHED, PENCIL-poised over paper with her back against the rough bark. She remembered the strangeness of the previous day.

Was it an odd coincidence, or had Kyan granted three wishes?

After the hubbub of the news crew and Eva Adams' social media blitz, the store had settled into a surreal quietude. While her uncle had walked to his office with stars in his eyes, Arianna slipped out and returned Kyan to his tree. The web hadn't been rebuilt, and he happily flitted into the twilight sky. To what realm did a talking dragonfly disappear?

An idea hit her.

Arianna bounded upright and began sketching, letting her imagination take flight. A womanly figure emerged with a gauzy dress and uneven hemlines. Fabric crisscrossed the bodice. The dress had a tapered waist with a gathered fabric sash.

Her back cramped, Arianna stretched out on the ground. She crossed her ankles, turning her face to the sun, momentarily basking in its golden warmth.

"You look beautiful," Kyan said.

She dropped her pencil in the grass. "You startled me."

Arianna bent forward, her long hair covering her hot face.

"I'm sorry."

"Thank you, Kyan." She glanced around, finding his iridescent blue body perched on her backpack.

"Don't let me interrupt you. Finish what you started." He waved a leg.

She grinned and picked up her pencil once more. She added wavy hair to the woman, deciding her model resembled Eva. Arianna shaded the drawing, bringing the sketch realism.

"It needs something more." She stared into the woods, tapping her lips with her eraser.

Kyan moved, his vibrating wings catching the sunlight.

"Oh," Arianna squeaked. She sat up and with a toothy smile. "Thank you, Kyan."

"You're welcome, my lady, for whatever help you've gleaned."

"It's the final touch." She pressed the charcoal tip to paper and lightly drew lines off the back of the gown. Tilting her head, her hair cascaded over her shoulders. She bit her lip, adding more shading while defining the woman's face. She nodded and sighed. "I think it's finished. What do you think?" Arianna turned the sketch toward him.

He twitched, rubbing a leg over a large compound eye, then stepped close. "This is brilliant. The lady looks alive. She's going to love your design."

"You inspired it," Arianna said. Careful not to jostle Kyan, she stowed the pad and pencil in her backpack.

"You are the inspiration, my love. Your light shines to all those around you, and we only reflect a portion." Kyan fluttered his wings, pressing them together over his back. "Except the Overlord; he is a mule who wears blinders."

The heat started on her face and spread across her chest. Emotion clogged her throat, but she managed to croak, "Thanks."

"What time are we working today?" Kyan rose and landed

on her arm. His gentle feet tickled the tender skin on her wrist. She tucked a stray curl behind her ear.

Arianna picked up the backpack with her free hand. "*We?*" She chuckled, walking toward the back door. "I'm probably late even if I'm not to start for two hours."

Kyan stomped around in a circle, then flew to her shoulder.

Arianna zipped to her workstation, setting her pad on the tabletop. She flipped to another design she'd drawn last night. Hopefully, Floyd would permit her to create it.

The entry door bell sounded repeatedly. Arianna peeked around the corner. Customers packed the store.

"What the…?" Arianna mouthed to Casey, who rung up a teenage girl with two giggling friends.

After the transaction, Casey ran her fingers through her hair. "Looks like the Evil Overlord got his wish. The slowest day of the week has been crazy. Your design is all over social media, and the locals are eating it up."

Casey's declaration conjured an image of teens chomping on cotton shirts, and Arianna laughed. "What can I do to help?"

"Nothing. Just go make more dragonfly T-shirts. I've got the register. John is somewhere over there putting out a few I made before the rush." She pointed toward the far front of the store, near the window. John popped his head up and waved.

"Hey, these things are selling as fast as we put them out," John called, folding another shirt.

"Where's Floyd?" Arianna asked.

Casey rolled her eyes and blew out a breath. "He's gone. Don't jinx us."

"Yeah, seriously." John walked to the register. "Casey and I are on the floor, helping, cleaning, and checking out the customers while you're in the sweat house."

Casey slapped John on the shoulder. "Not nice. It's her creation room."

"Whatever." He crinkled his nose. "It's hotter than Hades in that place. It's all you, Arianna."

"You better get busy, Arianna. Oh, here's a list of sizes people want. They'll be in sometime today. I told them after four."

"Wow." She took the paper, studying the names and sizing. "I can't believe people like my design."

"It's all Eva Adams' fault," Casey said. She waved her hand. "You better get a few made before Floyd gets back with the shipping supplies. Someone wants shirts shipped to California."

Dazed, Arianna shuffled into the backroom and stared at the machinery. After a moment, she squared her shoulders and began printing. She started with smalls, then mediums, until she had ten of each size.

Between printing, she took phone calls, adding to the list of pick ups. When her whistling uncle returned, he pranced up to her. "They like your bug shirt."

"It appears so," Arianna agreed, focusing on not getting burned. "I have another design on my desk if you'd like to look at it."

The phone rang, and the bell sounded in the other room. Floyd frowned. "Go ahead and make a few, but first answer the phone. I'll grab this pile for John to put out."

Arianna breathed easier once Floyd went to boss the others on the sales floor. "Hello?" she said into the old handset.

"Hi, is Mr. Floyd there?" a man inquired.

"Yes he is. Please hold and I'll get him—"

"No that's okay. I'm Eva Adams' personal assistant Geoffrey. She wants to visit the store and talk to a young lady named Arianna Travers."

"This is she." Arianna glanced at Kyan, who'd flown to the phone, landing on the glowing 7 key.

CHAPTER FIVE

SWEAT TRICKLED DOWN Arianna's aching back as she made another shirt. She couldn't guess the number she'd created already. The only plus side to the heat and exhaustion was that her uncle had embraced her designs, or at least the money they made.

Around two, her uncle slipped out to take his lunch. Arianna watched him climb into his Jeep as she dialed a number. "Yeah. He's gone, but I don't know how long he'll stay gone. Sometimes he brings the food back to eat." She hung up with a wide grin.

"What's that look?" Casey asked when Arianna slipped onto the sales floor.

"Eva Adams is coming, but she wanted to make sure my uncle wasn't here." Arianna finger-combed her long hair.

"Yeah, I get that. He was totally crushing on her." Casey laughed, then leaned to whisper, "Schmoozing is not his specialty. He went from gushing about her career and beauty to trying to sell the accolades of the store, namely you, I think. I see why she's avoiding him."

"Clever," Kyan said from somewhere behind Arianna.

She swallowed and nodded. "I try to avoid him too." Arianna caught her reflection off the glass. "I should pull my hair up. It's a mess." The bell rang while she was in the restroom freshening up. She returned to the checkout and gasped.

"You don't mind, do you?" Casey asked, red-faced.

"I... uh—"

"Of course she doesn't mind," Eva said with an illuminating smile. Her hair was swept up in a French twist and, *holy hell*, she wore Arianna's dragonfly shirt.

Arianna's gaze dropped from the shirt to the counter. Her sketchbook lay splayed open. She knew she stared and remained quiet too long, but words clogged her throat, unable to move around her heart. Her private ideas were exposed; this wasn't the way she wanted her designs to become known.

"I'm sorry," Casey mumbled. "She's very private," she aimed at Eva.

"You have nothing to worry about, my dear. You're very talented as an artist and a fashion designer." Eva tapped the corner of a page. "I'd put your work on my wall if I didn't want to wear it." She laughed, amused.

"Well, did you notice her new design when you came in?" Casey shot a sly glance at Arianna, then winked.

"Heavens no. I've got to see it." Eva sashayed after Casey, then gasped. "Oh my God. This is absolutely fabulous." She touched the material, then plucked a hanger up, lifting the design close to her face, inspecting. "Such detail," she murmured. She handed the shirt to Casey and sorted the sizes, searching for something more specific.

Handing those to Casey, Eva then took a photo of the design. "This is going on my social media." She grinned, becoming absorbed in her texting.

John sauntered up to Arianna and pinky-finger pointed toward the office. "He's back." He indicated with his head too, as if Arianna hadn't noticed.

"I'll go see how many blank shirts we have left in inventory," he said. "Maybe I can talk the Overlord into ordering more."

Arianna took a deep breath and closed her sketchbook. If Floyd caught her with it, he'd yell. She picked up the book, hugging it to herself.

"The woman Eva is correct, you do possess skill." Kyan landed on the book's binder.

"Geoffrey, check your phone, darling. I've sent another. Uh-huh." Eva swept her hand in the air as she twirled in place. "I know, right?" She laughed, then sobered when she glanced at Arianna.

"You won't be disappointed. See you soon. Gotta run, tah-tah." She air-kissed the phone, then stuffed it into her pocket.

Floyd shoulder bumped Arianna. "Why didn't somebody call me," he hissed, glaring at Arianna. A vein throbbed on his crimson forehead. His gaze dropped to the book in her hands. "I don't pay you to color."

Arianna's face grew hot, and she dropped her head, her hair cascading to hide her face. She twisted around, squeezing her eyes shut at the burn of moisture. She blinked, then ran from the room into the darkness of her work area.

Tossing the sketchbook to the table, she sighed and wiped her face. Floyd was beyond pissed. He would punish her. Extra hours. Unpaid, of course. She returned to the press and began churning out the novelty tees once more.

Fingers clamped onto Arianna's shoulders, sending shooting pain down her arms. "Oh," she squeaked.

Floyd spun her around and angled into her space. A big meaty hand with dagger-like fingers bit into her flesh. Onions and garlic lingered on his breath. "You better consider yourself lucky Eva likes you. Next time you waste time trying to sell your designs, you might not be so fortunate."

"But I didn't approach—"

"Consider yourself warned," he growled.

Arianna tried to shrug his hand off, but he smirked, tightening his grip. "You're hurting me," she whispered.

Out of the corner of her eye, a streak of blue dove at Floyd. *Kyan.* He buzzed Floyd's eyes, and her uncle jumped backward, releasing her. She rubbed her shoulder as Floyd danced around, waving his hands.

"What the hell is that thing?" Floyd ducked as Kyan dive-bombed him again.

"I think it has a stinger!" Arianna hollered. She hurried away from her uncle's reach.

Glancing back, she watched Floyd backhand Kyan. The dragonfly tumbled through the air and landed unmoving at Arianna's feet. She gasped, ripped a piece of paper from her sketchbook, and carefully slid it under his body to lift him.

"What was it? It was huge." Floyd righted his shirt and smoothed the remaining hairs on his head.

"Why don't you go check on Eva? I'll put it outside." Arianna turned away from her uncle.

"Just flush it," he yelled over his shoulder before grinning his used-car-salesman smile and disappearing onto the sales floor.

"Are you all right?" Arianna said, raising the paper to inspect Kyan. Two of his wings were bent at odd angles along with a few of his legs.

He groaned.

"What can I do to help?" she asked, as tears pricked her eyes for the second time that day.

Like the sound of a gentle breeze through the leaves, Kyan said, "The tree. I need to get back to the tree."

CHAPTER SIX

ARIANNA HURRIED INTO the glen behind the strip mall, attentive to watch her step and not jostle Kyan. She approached the tree that had once held the spiderweb.

"Up there," he said, pointing with an oddly bent leg.

Arianna glanced above her head to the thick limb that extended like a Y. She swallowed and searched for a way to reach the branch. On the back side of the tree, a limb the diameter of her arm offered hope.

"If I can only get up onto that branch," she mumbled, pressing her lips together. She scanned Kyan, and her heart lurched. He seemed so fragile and lifeless. She was sure Kyan couldn't see. It appeared the light had dimmed in his large eyes.

"I'm going to move you." She raised him onto her head from the paper. Once on top, she took a few strands of hair from either side of him then braided it loosely over him, securing him. She folded the paper and slipped it into her back pocket.

Hands free, she jumped, grabbing the branch and then walked her feet up the trunk until she could hook her knee around it. She pulled herself up, wiping the debris on her shirt. Precariously balancing, she proceeded to stand and reached for another branch toward the right. The limbs stair-stepped around the tree until she neared the other side. She sat near the split, noticing a hole in the bark had a slight shimmer. At first she froze, thinking honey caught the sunlight.

"Gateway," Kyan uttered. His slight movement tickled Arianna's scalp, sending tingles down her spine. She retrieved and unfolded the paper. Arianna gently unbraided her hair and let it fall, then tipped her head so Kyan could crawl into the paper. Lowering it to the trunk, he inched toward the light.

The shimmering reminded her of golden glitter-covered taffeta, and the longer she stared, the more it dissolved into a picture of another forest. Another world? She leaned, trying to see more.

Kyan reached the opening, and it sparkled. The portal slurped him and the paper in like a piece of spaghetti.

"Kyan!" Arianna shouted. Her heart lurched to her throat.

Bright light erupted, blinding Arianna. She gasped and reeled backward. Her grasp slipped, but she caught herself before tumbling out of the tree. The light began to wane, and she focused past the brightness. The forest canopy came into view, and she pinpointed a moving dark shape in the sky. Flesh color flashed, blocking the trees, and brought her focus back to where Kyan had vanished.

Tears threatened to spill. "Kyan?" Arianna whispered, reaching fingers to the hole's glowing cover.

"I wouldn't touch that if I were you," a deep voice rumbled.

Arianna froze, inspecting the other side searching for a speck of blue. "Kyan?" Dull heat throbbed from the opening.

"No." An amber basketball-sized eyeball stared at her. "I am his brother." A scaly black lid covered the eye in a monstrous wink.

Arianna's brain stalled as questions piled up, forming a traffic jam. She shook her head. "Kyan? Where is he? Is he all right? I can't see him. What happened? Is he hurt?"

The head moved backward, and a snout, a reptilian maw,

26

leered, exposing razor-sharp teeth. He snorted, and the gust nearly unseated her. She squeezed her thighs on either side of the branch, holding on.

Arianna gritted her teeth. Fear for her friend overrode the urge to flee. To save her, Kyan had attacked her uncle. Could she offer no less protection? "Where is he?" she demanded.

The beast tilted his head, and a clear lid slid over the bulbous amber. "Why do you care?"

Arianna's heart thumped as if trying to escape. Chin up, she declared, "He's my friend."

The creature raised his long serpentine head, glancing around, then stared at the ground.

"Please help him. Kyan is small and fragile." She sighed. The beast closed in on her again, and a surge of hope filled her. "He's a dragon—"

"Yes." He nodded and twisted, revealing a giant dinosaur-like body, with ebony scales, wicked dark talons, and a ridge of plates along his spine.

She blinked, then shook her head. "This isn't real," she breathed.

The beast lowered but kept his scaly back to her, blocking most of the view. He reached down then whipped around, his eyes like fire. "What have you done to him?" the dragon roared. Every word rumbled and vibrated the tree.

Arianna steadied her hands, her heart in her throat. She cocked her head, glancing past the monstrous black body. Unable to locate Kyan and certain the creature couldn't fit through the portal hole, she gathered her strength and stared into the large fiery eye. "Who are you?"

The beast snorted again. "I'm Jett, Kyan's brother."

"His brother? That doesn't make any sense." Arianna shook her head again. "Never mind that, do you see him?"

Jett emitted a low rumble, sounding like a cat purring. Although it must have been a growl.

"Please, Jett?" Tears welled in her eyes. "Kyan was protecting me from my uncle. His wings were bent oddly, and he didn't look good." She swiped at a renegade tear.

"He's on the forest floor." Jett shifted his head as if listening. "Yes, the girl is still here, and she's crying again."

"Kyan?" Arianna called past Jett's hulking mass.

"Fine." Jett moved away from the branch, opening the vista for her. He lowered his bulk until only the tip of his spiky back was visible.

A violet crow-like bird settled on a whitish branch of another tree, watching them. Arianna had never seen such a vibrant colored bird. There was no such bird locally or in North America. She found it hard to believe.

"What is this place?" she whispered. Magical talking dragonflies and dragons, strange birds, and weird colored trees.

"It's my home," a weak voice replied from somewhere unseen.

Arianna held her breath as Jett surged upward. In his claw he clasped a man. He maneuvered slowly so the man was protected from biting twigs. The guy's chest was bare, and the breeze blew his hair, cloaking his features.

"Oh," she squeaked, realizing he wore no clothing whatsoever. Toned and tanned, his physique mesmerized her. Jett's talon covered the man's manly-bits.

"Who is this?" Arianna stammered.

Jett's menacing grin exposed rows of pointed teeth. "My brother, Kyan."

"Wait. What?" Arianna rubbed her face.

Kyan reached for a limb and held it as Jett set his feet on a branch out of her sightline, then released him. He brushed his hair away from his face. Kyan's eyes sought hers. A huge gash streaked his forehead.

She gasped, leaning away from the portal. His irises were the same amazing shade of blue as Kyan the dragonfly. As she watched, the gash closed then disappeared. "What the…?"

CHAPTER SEVEN

I STUDIED ARIANNA'S delicate features, much like a porcelain figurine. Her silver eyes sparkled, reflecting the portal's magic. Her lips formed words, yet she uttered no sound.

"Arianna, are you well?" I asked. I steadied my footing and stepped closer to the portal. My right ankle tingled as my body healed.

She sighed and leaned in, her face dimly illuminated from the magical glow. Her dainty brows dipped as she inspected me. I could only guess what emotions toyed with her heart.

Jett's head loomed above me. While I appreciated my older brother's protectiveness, I wished he would scram. I desired a confidential conversation with my love.

Arianna's rosebud lips parted just as Jett sneezed, nearly knocking me out of the tree. I gripped the limb as my heart thundered. Her mouth snapped shut and her eyes widened.

"Leave us," I ordered Jett.

"But, brother—" Jett lowered his head to my eye level.

I pointed toward the sky, and Jett's head drooped. "I've already been maimed once today. Take off before your hot windedness is the death of me," I continued, "or you coat me with snot in front of my lady." I grinned at him.

Jett tilted his head, narrowing his eyes. "Do not tempt me, little brother. I will leave you. For now. Call if you need me."

Jett snorted, ruffling my hair, then jumped into the sky when I tried to slap him.

"Just wait until you meet your mate," I mumbled, but the big lizard had gone.

"Are you really brothers?" Arianna's thin voice drifted on the wind.

I loosed my grasp and sidled to the portal. "Yes."

"But he is a..." Her mouth bowed downward.

My stomach gurgled. Would she believe in dragons? Could she accept me for who and what I am? My tongue stuck to the roof of my mouth.

"Dragon? He said you are too. How can you be the Kyan I know? He was a little dragonfly," she waved her hand, "not a giant dinosaur or a hot guy."

Hot guy? My head buzzed and my face ached with the smile planted there.

"Why are you naked?" Arianna's voice cut through the fog of happiness.

"Oh." I glanced down at my body, knowing she could only see my upper half. "It's a shifter thing."

"Go on." She twirled her hand again, inviting me to continue.

"Here in Anaglacia in the kingdom of Ellehcor, I am either a dragon or a man. I wear clothes as a man, but it isn't feasible as a dragon. When I travel to your world, the magic transforms me into a dragonfly. No trousers needed." I paused, letting her absorb the information.

"What about your wounds? I know my uncle broke your wings and God knows what else. There was a cut above your eyes, and it disappeared." She shook her head, her silky blond hair tumbling over her shoulders.

"Shifters heal quickly here." I rubbed my head where the mending skin itched.

"But not in my world," Arianna said, then frowned. "You could have died, Kyan."

Hearing her utter my name, knowing my true form, made

the fire stir within. Stretching my fingers, I longed to touch her.

"I could not let the Overlord harm you." I balled my fist, the fire churning again, but this time in anger.

"Thank you." Arianna glanced down at her hands.

"How is your shoulder?" Concern saturated my words. She only shrugged, and I felt as if I'd consumed lead. "Arianna, show me your shoulder."

She drew a few deep breaths, continuing to study the bark of the branch on which she sat. "Arianna," I uttered, my dragon rumbling its fear.

Her head shot up and, wide-eyed, she met my gaze. "Please?" I tried again, stifling my dragon.

With a nod, she straightened and pulled her hair back. She stretched the neck of her shirt aside, exposing her flesh with angry red finger impressions.

I clamped my hands on the branch, willing my dragon to calm. Frightening Arianna wasn't what I wanted. She'd already been through so much.

"You're glowing," she gasped. "What's wrong?"

"I'm angry," I growled, heat burning my throat. "How can your uncle do that to you? You've been nothing but kind and helpful. Your creative skill is causing his business to thrive. He is your family, and the man is charged to care for you." The tips of my nails curled, biting into the bark. I stole a deep breath.

"He's a sad lonely man." Arianna glanced toward the shop. "My father ran off, abandoning my mom and I when I was young. Then my mother disappeared without a trace. My grandparents are all gone, so that left my uncle. He did his best."

"His best sucks," I grunted.

Arianna threw her head back and laughed. Instantly, my darkness lifted, and I chuckled. "What can you do to him as a dragonfly? Dive bomb him again?" She giggled.

I shrugged and suggested, "I could poop in his coffee."

Arianna's hands covered her mouth, and she shrieked. Her shoulders shook in time with her laughter. "I wish you could."

"Unfortunately, I am here. I can only grant your wishes when I am in your world." I glanced around. A large purple bird perched in a tree opposite the gateway. It was unlike anything I'd seen before. Could it have come through the portal?

Once she sobered, Arianna turned introspective. "You were very brave to face him. When I picked you up, I was as crushed as you were. I told my uncle I thought you could sting. It scared him. Serves him right too." With a stiff nod, she crossed her arms.

All I recalled of the incident was blinding pain. Between labored breaths, I'd tried to speak. My head had throbbed and fire crept down my back.

"Can I see?" Arianna asked, a pretty blush blooming over her cheeks.

My heart stalled. I couldn't speak; my mouth was suddenly as dry as the Sand Sea.

"The dragon part of you." She put her hands together as if praying. "Please?"

I dipped my head, hiding my face. If I wanted, I could ignore her request, jump from the tree, shift and fly home as my brother had. I turned away from the portal, knowing I could never refuse my mate.

CHAPTER EIGHT

ARIANNA'S PENCIL FLEW over the paper as the design blossomed on the page. A man sprouted dragon wings. He faced away, his profile illuminated by the full moon as he gazed heavenward.

"Oh my God, that's gorgeous!" Casey gushed from over Arianna's shoulder.

"Yes, he his." Heat crept from her chest to her face, and Arianna lowered her head, hiding the blush. Kyan remained hidden, sitting in a plant she'd bought for her workstation.

"The Evil Overlord just rented more space in the plaza." Casey plopped on a stool next to Arianna and began eating her lunch.

"What?" Arianna turned to her friend.

"Uh huh," she said through a mouthful.

Floyd burst into the room with a bright smile. Arianna nearly fell out of her seat. She'd never seen him so full of genuine joy. "Good news! Great news, actually."

He strutted around the women. When he came full circle, he jumped, clicking his heels. Arianna and Casey shared a look and a smirk.

"The landlord has agreed to rent the other half of the plaza to me. We are expanding." Floyd clapped his hands. "I have interviews this afternoon."

"With Eva Adams?" Arianna asked.

"Pfft. No, you dunce, I'm hiring more employees. I need to get them trained before we open up the new showroom."

"What about the current store?" Arianna asked.

"That space is for you, my dear niece. You will have the room to color. I plan on hiring people to make your shirts or whatever you plan to put the designs on." He rolled back on his heels, his grin unusually wide. "Hats, socks, leggings, scarves, the more the better."

Arianna stared at the machinery. They only needed one person to run the press and maybe another to help hang the merchandise. It was silly to think they could fill the store room even if they worked day and night. But reminding Floyd while he was so giddy probably wasn't a brilliant idea.

"The orders are pouring in. We will have an online store opening next week. The old store will also be the shipping department." He rubbed his hands together.

"It's all thanks to your magic wish-granting friend, my dear." Floyd leaned close, his onion breath offending her sensitive nose. "Things are looking good. People like your drawings. I don't know why, but they do. And as long as they are buying your designs, we will sell them. What's good for the business, is good for you."

"So, you'd like me to design full-time?" Arianna hesitated in hoping. She swallowed and shot a glance at Kyan's hiding spot.

The smile fell off Floyd's face, and with his hands on his hips, he frowned. "Didn't you hear me, girl?"

Arianna nodded. "I heard you. It's just so much good news. I'm overwhelmed."

"I know. Things are looking up for the first time since my loser stepbrother ran off, and well..." Floyd tapped his chin. "Anyway, you'll have a team to help you or whatever as long as the designs keep coming." He glanced at his watch, then turned on his heel and strode away.

Arianna returned to her seat and rubbed her face. How

would she keep up with the demand?

"Congratulations. I can't believe it. I think you were just promoted," Casey said, then popped a chip into her mouth.

"This is so much to digest." Arianna stared down at the man in her sketch and picked up her pencil again. "Drawing gives me pleasure. I love creating new things, but I don't want it to become a chore."

"I don't think it's a choice now." Casey shrugged, balling up her trash. She waved as she returned to the sales floor.

Arianna's heart thumped a happy beat, and she closed her eyes, letting her mind wander to the afternoon when she'd met the real Kyan. His perfectly chiseled torso. His intelligent eyes that sparkled like the Caribbean Sea. His thick brown dragon-blown hair. His flirty smile. He treated her with respect and had answered her questions patiently. Then he'd shifted.

A tickle on her finger. Her eyes popped open. Poised on her pencil, Kyan caressed her finger with two of his little legs. Maybe she wanted to believe he caressed her.

"Are you well?" Kyan asked, tilting his head.

Arianna sighed. "I don't know. Maybe I'm going crazy. I'm having a conversation with an insect who really isn't an insect, and I think my uncle is happy."

"You aren't crazy, Arianna." He lifted off the pencil and floated before her at eye level. "Never think that way."

Tears stung her eyes, and she bobbed her head. "Thank you. I don't know what I did to deserve a friend like you."

"A friend?" he repeated, landing next to the image of his other self. He touched the highlight lines she'd added to his hair.

Arianna daydreamed about the dragon-man. Thinking of him made her insides warm, kind of like a dragon. She giggled. "What do you think? Should I add something?" She glanced down at the sketch on her desk.

"Clothes, perhaps." Kyan walked over to the paper, covering his derrière.

"Don't you think it's a good likeness?" she asked, adding detail to the moon.

"Would you share me with the world?" He rose and retreated to the plant.

Arianna froze with her pencil to the paper. Her jaw dropped but slowly shut. No. She wouldn't share her memory or Kyan's glorious body with anyone.

Suddenly her pencil was flying once more. She added lines at his neck and wrists. Then drew pants with a belt. The man frolicked barefoot along still water, which reflected the moon. Fireflies dotted the pathway and night sky.

Kyan poked his head out from behind a leaf. "Are my ears that pointed?"

"No." She chewed her lip as she made final touches on the man's clothing. She set the pencil aside with a smile. "I exaggerated them slightly," she admitted. "He's an elf."

"Is that what you call my kind in this world?" he asked.

"It depends." She pulled out a clean sheet of paper, then sharpened her pencil.

"On what?" Kyan had crawled from under the leaf and clung to the edge of the pot.

"If they're from outer space." Arianna sketched a teardrop shape.

"Harrumph."

"No really. Pointy-eared people from space are either Vulcans or Romulans. Elves or fairies have pointed ears too, but they usually live in the woodlands. Here, or in another realm." She glanced up. "I suppose you would be considered an elf, but they're fictional. Or at least, I used to think so."

Kyan buzzed to her nose and grabbed it. Cross eyed, she focused on the blue blur. His body began to glow, heating her nose. "I am real."

"I know," she breathed, closing her eyes and envisioning his nude body sprouting wings and a tail. Even in the dim forest light, she had known his scales to be the same blue as his dragonfly form. When he faced her fully transformed, she could find no words. He was magnificent. Kyan's eyes had appeared to beg for acceptance. Arianna had been overwhelmed with the desire to fall into Kyan's world and into his arms.

The warmth moved up the bridge of her nose, his glow penetrating her eyelids. She instinctively raised her hand, sliding her finger along her nose until she touched him.

His wings fluttered, fanning her face. "Arianna." His timbre made her shiver. The dragon had called to her with the same longing.

Floyd stomped up from behind her, and Kyan fled. Her uncle grabbed her shoulder forcefully, making her wince. "Tell the magic bug I wish that local rap star Pryce T. A. G. would make a ditty for a commercial for the shop."

Arianna jumped up, effectively breaking free from her uncle's grasp. She glared at him.

"Remember, girl, what's good for the store is good for you."

CHAPTER NINE

"WELL, WHAT DOES he want now?" Kyan buzzed around Arianna's head, wreathing it.

"You know, the usual." Arianna glanced around the old store, now empty except for the construction crew. "Look at this place. It's so barren without all the fixtures." Plastic covered a glass door into the new store. The shiny chrome racks held merchandise organized by schools, colors, and styles. Her newest creation was featured in the windows, drawing the customers inside.

The back wall appeared to be reclaimed brick and the floors old wood, but the building had been built in the 70s. The vintage warehouse style with high ceilings and exposed ductwork made the room appear vast. The new unisex fitting rooms with rolling barn doors had ample space to try things on.

Casey had been promoted to assistant manager. She trained a new employee behind the long customer service station. John and another newbie greeted customers, put out stock and straightened the floor.

"Ms. Travers," a man called. His yellow hardhat tipped slightly toward the right. He pushed up his safety glasses. His big bushy mustache couldn't hide his grin. "I'm Bart O'Donnell, and I have a question for you. It's about your office."

Kyan settled in her hair.

"Yes, sir?"

"Mr. Floyd told me you'd like the old fitting room to remain the same size?" He pointed to the dingy walls in the corner.

"Oh, heavens no," a thin black man declared, striding over to Arianna. He extended his hand. "Listen, Ms. Travers, your uncle asked me to get your space in order. I'm going to give you an organized workspace. All you'll have to do is come in here and create."

"Who are you?" Arianna asked. She scanned him as he straightened his bowtie. Darius could have stepped out of an episode of *Queer Eye* either as a transformed guest or soigné host.

"Darius Jones. I am your personal assistant." He stood back with a hand on his hip and a finger on his chin. "Hmm. We need to talk about your wardrobe."

Arianna gasped and met Bart's gaze. He shook his head.

"It can wait for now. As to the office, that box won't do. Freedom of thought takes open space." Darius spread his arms wide.

"I'd like that corner," Arianna said, but lifted her finger to silence Darius's pout. "I want the glass fire emergency door in my office. It lets in natural light, and nature inspires me. I'd like to be able to exit, if possible, from there. There's a forest behind the building, and it's peaceful. I sketch there a lot."

"Inspiration is good." Darius nodded. "I can work with that."

Watching the negotiations between Darius and Bart, while sporting, had drained Arianna. She longed to escape to her wooded oasis and bask in the sun's warmth and light. Spotting her backpack near the old press, she edged toward it. She stifled a yawn and stepped backward.

Darius stepped around Bart and wagged his finger. "Oh no you don't. We've got work to do, Ms. Travers."

Arianna swallowed and inhaled. "So much for escaping," she mumbled.

Darius pushed up his stylish glasses and speed-walked to her side. "I'd like to see your work."

Arianna pursed her lips, biting back the shock and anger. She twirled and picked up the backpack.

"Ms. Travers?" Darius called, trailing her. Arianna reached the back door and pushed it open.

"Stop!" Floyd called.

Arianna swung an exasperated gaze at her uncle and paused, holding her breath.

"I see you've met Darius. He's here to keep you organized." Floyd motioned to Darius. "You know these creative types?" He laughed.

"If you'd like to see my sketchbook then come with me." Arianna walked out, not caring if the stranger followed. She blinked in the bright light but strolled to her favorite tree. The crunching of hurried steps behind her announced her shadow.

She hesitated, examining her patch of heaven. Kyan hovered near her drawing tree. She sighed and continued forward. She plopped her bag down, then sat cross-legged. Arianna glanced up and patted the ground beside her.

Darius scooted close as she opened the backpack and retrieved her sketchpad. He accepted it as if she handed him gold. He glanced at her with a wide smile. "Thank you, Ms. Travers."

Darius flipped the first page. "Oh." He reacted similarly to the others with an "Ah, um, or uh, huh." Once he turned the page sideways and hummed, "nice."

Arianna chewed her lip. Her stomach gurgled as if she was being judged by an art critic.

Darius took off his glasses and rubbed his eyes. "I think we'll need at least three seamstresses." His cognac colored eyes studied the clouds.

"What?" Arianna wasn't sure she'd heard him correctly.

"We already have an embroidery machine. You punch in the design, set it, and go. It's pretty automated."

Darius tapped her book. "Sure, there are many drawings that will work for embroidery or silkscreen, but there are others that need to be made." He flipped the sketchbook open to the lady wearing the dragonfly wings. "This one. It's going to be a hit at Halloween. Ms. Adams told me you had talent, and she's right. We are going to make you a name brand."

Arianna rubbed her forehead. Was this too much too soon, or a dream come true? "Thanks, but good luck getting my uncle to spend the money."

Darius tilted his head and cracked his knuckles. "Let me work my magic," he said with an impish grin.

Arianna chuckled. "I can't wait to see it."

"Now, let me see your other stuff. I know you've got to keep more than one design book." Darius pointed to her bag.

Sure, she had other books. Many of the drawings were nothing more than doodles, but she'd made a fair share of Kyan in dragon and man form. She'd also drawn a few of Kyan and her together. Fanciful drawings from the heart. She hadn't shown them to anyone. Arianna's gaze darted around, searching for Kyan.

"Please?" Darius rose to his knees and touched her arm.

She sighed and nodded. First, she'd found her fashion sketchpad and handed it over. As Darius flipped the pages humming, Arianna reached for her treasure. Hidden within the inner pocket was a smaller notepad. She fingered the spiral binding and then fished it out. She held it with both hands but released it when he tugged on it.

"Oh, heavens." Darius fanned himself. "This creature is gorgeous." He pointed to a portrait of Kyan.

Arianna suddenly liked Darius. "He's beautiful," she murmured.

"This is the store's ticket to notoriety." Darius waved the book in the air. "These are fantabulous. Of course, there's so much to do before we are anywhere near producing anything of this caliber."

Arianna snatched the notebook back and hid it away. "Those are mine. I don't want to share them."

"Not yet." Darius stood, dusting off his rear and legs. "From now on your signature needs to be on each drawing. Incorporate it into the design, if you can. Okay. It's a start." He nodded, rubbing his hands together. He popped up, her fashion sketch pad under his arm, and headed toward the store. "And let's talk about what you are wearing," he threw over his shoulder.

Arianna frowned with a hand on her hips. "And what's wrong with my clothes?"

CHAPTER TEN

ARIANNA SLID OFF her stool and arched her back. The new drafting table helped her keep several designs in front of her at once. She paced circles around the desk.

"Knock knock." Darius announced his presence before sashaying in. "Arianna, won't you give Maud a minute of your time?" He puckered his lips into a pouty face and batted his eyelashes.

Arianna covered her mouth and giggled. His silly-face never failed to make her laugh. "What now?"

"You know." He rolled his cognac eyes. "She'll be in to measure for this." He slapped a paper on the tabletop.

Arianna recognized her design. She adored the sleeveless white scoop-necked shirt, paired with the blue skirt. It was classy yet modern. It was one of six drawings that Darius had taken and enlarged. He had them matted in white then framed in black. Darius had Bart hang the three on the wall. The other three hung in the waiting area outside her office.

"Ms. Travers?" One blue-shadowed eye peeked into the room. A pencil stuck out of Maud's mousy-brown permed fro.

"Come on in, Maud, before Darius pushes you inside." Arianna waved her in.

Maud nodded, staring at her shoes as she approached. Her

petite size bordered on frail. "I need to take your measurements." She fingered a baby blue fabric measuring tape.

"What exactly are we making?" Arianna cocked her head, glancing at the designs on the wall.

Maud studied her hands. "I think he wants me to make all of them."

Arianna rubbed her forehead. "Lordy."

Maud's head shot up, and she met Arianna's gaze. "I can make them. Don't worry about that."

"I wasn't talking about your skill, Maud. Darius can be bossy." Arianna glanced over toward her plant. A flash of blue.

"I heard that," Darius said, whisking in. "Let's get you measured. Maud needs to get started on your new wardrobe. You have appointments with Eva Adams next week and one of her cronies, and I want you stylin' and profilin'."

Arianna lifted her arms and Maud measured her waist, hips, then bust. As she measured, she called out numbers and Darius recorded them on a notepad. Maud turned Arianna around.

"You can drop your arms. We're almost done." Maud smiled at the conclusion. "What material do you want for this?" She tapped the picture Darius had laid out earlier.

"You mean Darius hasn't figured it out yet?" Arianna asked in mock shock.

"Oh heavens no. Not my department." He crossed his arms.

Arianna winked at Maud, whose lopsided smirk was the first smile Arianna had seen. "I thought everything fell into your department."

He narrowed his eyes and waggled a finger. "How much time in the day do you think I have? I've got to leave some things to you ladies." Darius straightened his purple bowtie. "But a moire would be nice for the skirt."

Arianna giggled. "I knew it."

"I always have ideas." Darius grinned.

"In this instance, I will defer to the expert." Arianna pointed to Maud.

"Me?" Maud took a step back. "But surely you know what you want for your designs."

Arianna lifted a pencil and inspected the tip. "I drew it with a vague idea for the colors. I wasn't thinking silk versus denim. Not for this picture. It was about the style." She tapped the drawing. "I trust Darius, and he picked you, Maud, as the best. You have the freedom to choose the fabrics. I'd like them to be soft and washable. I like to sit outside."

Darius pointed the notepad at Arianna. "She's not joking. This lady loves her mother. Mother Nature, that is."

A pang of longing stabbed Arianna's heart. She had loved her mom, even though she'd vanished. Arianna sighed and glanced at the paper, trying to blink away the tears. A blur of blue caught her eye again. Kyan leaned out of his cover of the plant.

Arianna couldn't risk his exposure. She sucked in a cleansing breath and rolled her shoulders. "I love this outfit. I can't wait to see you work your magic, Maud."

Darius' Cheshire Cat smile widened as Maud nodded. She slipped out of the room, and Darius waited until Maud was out of earshot. "About Eva's gown or costume..." He waved his hand. "I have Diana searching the internet for wings. You don't know what's on the internet until you research something. There are fairy wings, bat wings, bird, butterfly, and dragonfly wings. Dragon wings too." Darius rubbed his chin.

"I'm sure she indicated dragonfly wings." Arianna flipped through her sketchbook, pointing to the drawing that started the store's transformation.

Darius glanced over her shoulder to the design. "Yes. I know, but she has access to the internet too."

"Arianna's designs aren't on the internet," Floyd said. Darius' hand jumped to cover his heart. Floyd continued,

"Remind Eva and her cronies of that, Darius. They need to be mindful of Arianna's time. Her designs are exclusive. They aren't some internet knockoff."

Arianna smiled. Her uncle had never defended her before. Warmth pooled in her chest.

Darius saluted Floyd. "It's good to know."

"Exclusivities are money just like time is money." Floyd grinned with a wink, then vanished.

The warmth dissipated as fast as Floyd had disappeared. She rubbed her heart, trying to relieve the ache. She resumed her place on her stool and doodled on a blank page.

"I'll notify Ms. Adams of your uncle's stipulations, then I'll see how Maud and Diana are doing. Shout or text if you need anything."

Arianna raised a hand to acknowledge she'd heard, but kept drawing circles. When the sound of his dress shoes clacking softened, she drooped with a sigh.

"What troubles you, my love?" Kyan landed on the end of her pencil.

She squeezed her eyes shut, the ache returning. Her hair curtained her face. "I miss," her voice warbled, "my mom and grandparents." She studied his iridescent wings.

"You are loved, remember that." Kyan tilted his head. The little dragonflies in her stomach took flight as she imagined his man form.

"You are lucky you have a family."

Kyan bobbed his head. He had Jett, Falun, Zaffrie, and other siblings as well as living parents. "It's true. I have numerous family members. When you're royalty, many claim to be your cousins. Trust me. More is not always better."

"Royalty?" Arianna's mouth became dry, and she reached for a water bottle.

His little front arm waved. "Yes. With all the pomp and obligatory tasks and events. Regulations about behavior and such."

"Oh." She sat up. *Did dragons wear crowns?* "Like balls?"

46

"Yes," he sighed. "We have several yearly, but none is like the Harvest Moon. It is the largest dance. All Ellehcor comes together. Friends are reunited and mates are selected."

Mates? She swallowed a surge of jealousy. Her eyes widened. "Oh, I'd die to see the gowns. The colors, styles, and material—"

"I must ask a favor of you." Kyan cleared his throat. "I am in need of your services. Could you find time to design my attire for the ball?"

CHAPTER ELEVEN

VISIONS OF KYAN in a tuxedo dominated Arianna's daydreams. She had agreed to his request, but she needed his non-dragonfly measurements.

Darius pressed his lips together, tapping his foot. He hadn't believed her when she'd announced a royal wanted her to design formal attire.

"Come on, Darius, I need your help. Women's fashion is my thing," Arianna pleaded.

"I haven't met him. You have. What's your take? Did he give a modern, classic, or retro vibe? Black, gray, or white?" He straightened his bowtie, then opened his laptop, searching for men's formalwear. "Is his single?"

Arianna tapped her chin. "Leave that open, and let me think for a while." She stood and circled her desk.

"I'll check in with Maud and see how Eva Adams' dress is coming along. I'm sure Eva will want an update, anyway." Darius winked and left her office.

Kyan hovered near the screen. "This is similar to what we wear." He pointed to a tux with tails.

Arianna leaned in and enlarged the photo. It was a regency styled jacket. "I can work with this. Black hands down. White wing collar shirt with a cravat. Double-breasted waistcoat with satin edged lapels, maybe." She tapped her chin again.

Taking a fresh paper, she sketched a basic male frame, adding Kyan's hair curling around his ears. The cravat proved tricky to draw. As she touched up the tuxedo, Kyan murmured his approval. "I like it. How can you do this for me?"

"You'll need to measure for me while you're at home." Arianna approved of the tapered waist and athletic lines of his pants. Black leather shoes finished the look.

"I have boots," Kyan said, "But I like these shoes. I'll be the only one with shoes like this."

"I can get them for you." She smiled. "I'll need your shoe size too." Arianna searched for instructions on how to measure. She printed one with diagrams. "I'll be right back."

Arianna skipped out of her office to Maud's work station. She had a garment upside-down. The older woman worked on piecing together a skirt. Another dress hung unfinished on a dress form.

"Do you have a spare fabric measuring tape?" Arianna asked.

Maud pointed to a drawer. "In there," she said around the pins in her mouth.

Arianna pulled open the drawer and found a box of the cloth measuring tapes rubber banded together. She took two. "Thanks."

Arianna retrieved a padded mailing envelope from the shipping room. She hurried to her office and shut the door behind her. Kyan buzzed near the glass window of the back door. He faced his tree.

Arianna glanced at the items in her hands. "Do you think there will be a problem with this stuff going through to your world?"

"No."

"But you change when you come here. Won't the energy or magic or whatever damage it?" She slid the printouts into the envelope.

Kyan flew close, hovering near her hand. "The items will

remain unharmed. I know this from last time the paper entered into my world."

Arianna glanced at her sketchbook, trying to recall a time there'd been a paper transfer. "Last time?"

"When you rescued me from the Overlord and delivered me to the tree, do you not remember you carried me upon a paper?" Kyan rose to her eye level. "The paper as well as the sketch drawn on it were unharmed. In fact, I shared your talent with my family."

"Oh." Heat flared on Arianna's cheeks, and she swiped her hair away from her face. The royals had seen one of her doodles. "Which sketch?"

"A woman in a stunning gown," Kyan said, floating toward the window once more. "Come, let's return to the tree so I can take the measurements for you."

Kyan's perfect derrière flashed in her mind, and Arianna smiled. With a deft swipe, she snatched the full envelope, cradling it to her chest. She placed it into her backpack, and they stole out the glass door, leaving the office behind.

She'd had many visits to the gateway, sitting on the branch while speaking with Kyan the man. Her stomach fluttered, knowing she'd see his face again soon. Arianna had learned that climbing a tree with a backpack was easier than hoisting herself up while holding something. She also kept a step stool near the base of the trunk.

As she reached the shimmering hole, she glanced through, noticing an amber light. "The sun is setting," Arianna said, settling onto her branch.

"It's morning light," Kyan replied, landing on her knee.

"Morning? Kyan, I'm sorry for messing with your sleep schedule." She frowned.

"I sleep better now that I dream of you." He turned around, tickling her knee.

She giggled, feeling the heat return. "You are so sweet."

Kyan tipped his head. "Let's put the envelope through." His wings blurred as he lifted off her leg and hovered near the opening. She retrieved the envelope and edged to the light. As she pressed it to the barrier, the magic caught it and slurped it in. Appearing intact, the envelope teetered on the branch momentarily before plunging out of sight.

"I'll see if its damaged." Kyan flew into the sparkling light, and it flashed. Arianna blinked, seeing a foot fly over the edge. A minute later, Kyan climbed the tree clothed with the envelope in hand. He pried it open and reached in. "I can do this now."

"There's no rush." Arianna watched his hands as they fingered the measuring tape. "I don't want you to fall out of the tree." Even though she'd just seen him plummet from the branch. She shook her head, recognizing she probably sounded foolish.

"Do not fret. I enter my world falling onto the forest floor. Arianna, I will take the packet, study the instructions, and get Jett, Falun, or one of my other brothers to assist me." He dropped the tape into the envelope, then leaned in toward the portal. His blue eyes mesmerized Arianna, and she forgot to breathe. "Do you approve of my attire?" His inviting lips tipped into a grin as he set the envelope on a twig with leaves.

Arianna reluctantly pulled her gaze from his face and scanned his white button-down shirt and tan trousers. "I can't say it's an improvement," she grumbled, missing his smooth, bare skin.

Kyan quirked an eyebrow. "What was that?"

"It's not as tempting to draw," she admitted, owning the redness on her cheeks. "Don't worry, I'll protect your modesty."

"Modesty?" Kyan threw his head backward and laughed. "I'm a shifter. Clothes are optional."

A slow burn ignited in Arianna's core, and she squirmed on the branch. "Why wear them now?" she teased with a smirk.

He fiddled with the top button, inviting her gaze. His lithe

51

fingers rubbed the pearlescent sphere. She swallowed and opened her mouth.

A noise, reminding Arianna of a truck taking a train track crossing too fast, resounded in the distance. She snapped her mouth shut and peered into the tree canopy behind Kyan.

He sighed and turned, examining the sky. "I apologize, Arianna."

CHAPTER TWELVE

"What is it?" The sound repeated at regular intervals, becoming louder each time. "Dragon wings?"

Kyan nodded, frowning.

"Is it Jett?" she asked.

"No." Leaning against the limb, he straightened his tunic and hastily tucked it into his pants. He finger-combed his hair, but some stuck up.

"Here." Arianna retrieved a small brush and pushed it through the portal. It popped through with a zap into his waiting hand. He ran it through his thick dark locks, parting his hair to the side.

"Thank you, my love." He winked.

Little dragonflies took flight in her stomach each time he called her love. Her hands flew to her cheeks. "I must be part dragon," she whispered.

He tilted his head, stepping closer. "What was it you said?" Brow furrowed, he scanned her face.

She pushed the words through her dry mouth. "I must be part dragon."

"You are part dragon? How can that be?" His intense sapphire gaze nailed her in place.

"I'm always hot on the inside." Arianna closed her eyes and inhaled deeply. She fanned herself, then glanced at her watch.

Too much longer and Darius would come searching for her latest drawing.

"You aren't glowing," Kyan said. Arianna giggled, and her gaze softened.

A great thump shook the forest. Several leaves drifted downward.

A white-gold dragon head snaked into view. The oval shape of the eyes and gentler, less angled slope of the snout hinted at a female. *Could this be Kyan's mate?* Without speaking, the dragon examined Kyan. Her gaze narrowed when she spotted Arianna. In a flash, she disappeared.

Kyan reached down and offered his hand. A woman with long hair the same color as Kyan's stepped onto the limb next to him. She wore a robe the same shimmery white-gold as her dragon's scales. The cuffs and collar had thick white fleece. Crow's feet framed her sapphire eyes. She stood regally, even though she was inches shorter than Kyan.

"Hello," Arianna said when she couldn't stand the silence any longer.

The woman's lips tipped into a half grin. "You were correct, Kyan. She is exquisite. She reminds me of someone." Her black waves shifted as she tilted her head.

"I'm glad you approve, Mother," he replied.

Arianna gasped, recognizing the similarities in the shape of their eyes. "Thank you," she responded, adding a smile.

"You are the seamstress?" Kyan's mother's laser-beam gaze narrowed on Arianna.

"Mother, she's not a simple seamstress. She's the creator of the designs." Kyan huffed. "Look at this." He opened the flap of the envelope and fished out his suit doodle.

"Hmm." She studied the paper, then Kyan. "I see."

"Excuse me." Arianna raised her hand. "What should I call you?"

"What do you call queens in your world?" Kyan's mother asked.

Arianna sat up straight. "Your Majesty or my lady, I guess."

She narrowed her gaze on Kyan. "Your mother is the queen and you didn't think to tell me? That means you're a prince." She laughed and rubbed her head.

"You failed to tell the girl? Shame, son."

"Why tell her? She has no queen over her. She has enough in her world to consider from her work to the Overlord," Kyan snapped at his mother.

Arianna reeled, gripping the branch. Kyan a prince. She bit her lip.

"Call me Nora," she instructed Arianna. "Since I am not your queen." Nora placed her hand on Kyan's arm. "You truly care for her. I see where your heart lies."

Kyan's lips tightened as he nodded.

The queen dropped her hand to a pocket in her robe. She pulled out a scrap of paper and unfolded it. "Daughter, will you make this for me?"

Daughter? Arianna inhaled sharply, and tears stung her eyes. She held up a finger as she blinked away the tears. She focused first on Kyan's face. His tender expression had the heat returning. She swallowed before examining the paper.

"Oh. It's my dress." Arianna grinned. "You like it?"

"It's divine. You are most talented." A grand smile spread over Nora's face. "I applaud your design."

Words failed Arianna. Her gaze volleyed from Kyan to Nora. Arianna tugged on her earlobe. "I didn't hear that right. A queen wants me to make a gown. Me. Holy moly." She rubbed her chest. "May I see the paper?"

Nora stretched her arm, lifting the paper toward the portal. Once the paper touched the magic energy it darkened, and a tendril of smoke wafted into the air. The queen jerked her hand away, saving the image from destruction.

"Is that what happens to objects from my world when you try to return them? What would happen to something alive, like me?" Arianna's heart grew heavy.

"The magic keeps the birds or bugs from returning. If you entered you could never go home." Kyan glanced at the smoking paper.

Arianna nodded with a sigh. She pulled out her sketchbook and a pencil. "Nora, could you please raise the paper as close as possible so I can copy it?" Arianna started with customizing Nora's shape, then recreated the lines of the gown. As she worked, she asked questions, trying to get a feel for Nora's style likes and dislikes.

Without stopping, Arianna said, "The skirt looks like flower petals, but it's not. The pattern is from monarch butterfly wings. The colors of a monarch are orange, black, and white. These colors are also prominent in my world's harvest celebrations. Would you like to use these colors, or would you prefer something more subtle?"

"I will defer to your wisdom," Nora said breathlessly.

Arianna glanced up and smiled. Nora watched with her nose practically pressing the magic barrier. Kyan rested his chin on his mother's shoulder and had wrapped his arm around her waist, holding her back. The tender scene between mother and son further heightened Arianna's resolve to create the perfect dress.

CHAPTER THIRTEEN

"Arianna," John said, poking his head inside her office. "I hate to bother you, but…"

"But what?" Arianna lifted her head, arching her back in a stretch.

"Casey told me to come get you. There's some dude in the store who won't go away until he talks to you." John stepped up to her side and studied the pencil sketch taped to the desk.

"What dude?" Arianna glanced at John.

"Garret or Jared. Something like that." John turned to inspect the framed wall art.

Arianna tried to swallow, but her mouth had gone dry. She wiped her palms on her skirt. "Did he mention going to school with me?"

John spun around with a grin. "Yes. So, who is this guy? Casey guessed he's an ex-boyfriend."

Arianna shook her head, causing her loose bun to fall out. "Nope. Nothing like that."

John thrust his hands into his front pockets. "Weird."

Arianna inhaled deeply and stymied a shiver. "We graduated together, but we weren't even friends."

John rolled back on his heels. "He's not the most honest fellow."

"As I recall, he was always a shyster. I bet he didn't

explicitly say we dated but implied it." Arianna crossed her arms.

"Exactly." John nodded.

"Tell Casey I'll be there in a few. Also, warn her." After John left, Arianna sat in silence. She hadn't thought of Jared since she'd graduated high school years ago. Jared had been the proverbial popular, handsome jock with the cheerleader girlfriend-of-the-week on his arm. He'd never paid any positive attention to nerds or shy people like her.

"My love?" Kyan leaned over the edge of the pot. "Why does this person trouble you?" Kyan canted his head.

"In school, Jared didn't care who he hurt with his comments or actions. It was all about making him look good. He had to get the laughs by bullying others." She frowned, thinking back to one event in particular. Lunch period had never been the same afterward.

"Why is he here now?" She asked the universe then sighed. "I better go see what he wants."

"I'll come with you." Kyan lifted out of the plant and flitted to her hand.

"I appreciate the support." Her heart lightened as she left the office.

A rush of cool air fluttered Kyan's wings as she pushed the door to the store. John rung up a customer at the cash register, and Casey had an embroidery catalog open at the counter. She flipped to a page, and the woman client smiled and nodded.

Arianna's scalp tingled as Kyan settled in her hair.

Arianna spotted Jared near the front. He examined the rack of shirts holding her most recent design. Jared's forehead had expanded and his athletic physique had morphed as if all the muscles gathered around his middle.

He glanced up and met her eyes. A huge smile flashed, exposing his signature dimples. The lack of anxiety at seeing him surprised Arianna. She'd expected to be intimidated, but she was only annoyed and, maybe, a smidge curious.

"Arianna, it's good to see you again." Jared reached for her small hands, covering them in his meaty damp ones.

"I'm surprised to see you here," she replied, pulling her hands out of his knuckle grinding grasp.

"I know." Jared laughed. "It took a while for you to come meet me." He almost pouted.

Arianna glanced at Casey, who made a fist and hit it in the palm of her other hand, causing Arianna to smile. "I'm busy. You came to the store seeking me out." *Not the other way around.* "Why are you here?"

Jared's lips flattened for a moment. He shifted closer, leaning into Arianna's space. "I'm here to make your dreams come true."

Arianna tossed her head back and laughed. "What do you know of my dreams?"

"I'd like to take you out," Jared replied, standing taller.

"No, thanks." Arianna turned to go, but Jared caught her hand.

"Wait." Jared said when she yanked her hand free.

"Is there a problem?" Casey asked, stepping beside Arianna. Her curly hair framed her heart-shaped face and, coupled with her frown, gave her the appearance of an angry poodle. She tapped her foot.

"No. Jared is leaving." Arianna glared, hoping he'd take the hint.

Jared applied the condescending smile Arianna remembered from school. "We are just getting started."

Heat spread over Arianna's face as anger built. She placed her hands on her hips. "Why are you here, Jared?"

"To ask—"

"Don't give me that date crap. Why are you here now? Why not years ago?" Arianna pegged Jared with a stare.

"I…" Jared started but glanced at the flatscreen on the wall.

"You what?"

"I saw you on TV."

"And there it is," Casey said, folding her arms over her

chest. "There's the truth."

"Yeah. I saw you and thought you looked pretty. So here I am. I thought we could reminisce about the good ol' days." Jared shrugged. "I assumed you'd like to go out with me."

"Why would she do that?" Casey asked. "She was nothing to you back then, and suddenly she's the talk of the town, and, low and behold, you show up."

Jared's mouth hung open, and his cheeks flamed red.

Arianna touched Casey's arm, quelling her impassioned friend. "Casey makes a great observation. Let me expand upon it for you, Jared. Despite what you think, not every girl in school had a crush on you. And high school wasn't my glory days. I couldn't wait to graduate, and it was thanks to bullies like you."

Jared frowned. "Hold on a minute. I wouldn't—"

Casey rolled her eyes.

"You said I was unlovable, and that's why my parents didn't want me and left." Arianna remembered the other student's stares. "It wasn't anyone's business whether I was an orphan, yet you kept announcing it any chance you could. I already missed my parents, and you kept trying to make me feel as if their actions were my fault. Why would you torment a lonely girl?"

Kyan gasped and his body warmed.

John, who'd been eavesdropping while folding shirts on a nearby table, grumbled at Jared, "Man, you're a loser."

"Arianna is one of the sweetest people on this planet." Casey shook her head.

Jared shifted from side to side. His ability to score touchdowns could not cover for his behavior any longer.

Arianna's view of Jared drifted from menacing ruffian to a washed-up has been.

"Listen Jared, I understand back then you had issues with your identity. All bullies do. They point out other people's flaws to keep their own hidden. I knew it back then, and I know it today. Just because I'm able to realize why you did what you did doesn't mean I've forgotten." Arianna glanced at Casey and John.

"And it doesn't mean I'd trust going out with someone who belittled me." Arianna smiled and linked arms with Casey.

"My father was a bully. He used to call my mother horrible things. She always cried. One day he took off with a younger woman. My mom prayed for that lady, knowing when the newness wore off Dad would start belittling her too. After he left, we had peace. My mother was a courageous woman, and she loved and protected me. It devastated me when she disappeared." Arianna swallowed the lump in her throat. "We don't know where she is…"

"The Overlord says your dad returned to nix her," Casey offered in a small voice.

"There's no proof." Arianna glanced out the window. "I like to pretend she's happy and living someplace beautiful."

"I'm sorry about your parents." Jared cleared his throat. "I never knew."

Arianna met his eyes once more and nodded.

Darius opened the office door. "There you are," he called with a wave. "Your next client is here."

"I'll be there in a minute." Arianna sighed. "I need to go."

Jared glanced at his hands. "I'm sorry."

"If you really are sorry, then you should offer support to the people you've hurt," Casey suggested.

Arianna smiled. "Great idea. Lyndsay Davis has a gym—"

"The Amazon." Jared offered the name he'd used.

"And Terry Bradshaw is an accountant." Arianna rubbed her chin, trying to think of what careers some of the others had chosen.

"Machine Gun," Jared said with a laugh.

Arianna frowned and told Casey. "The poor guy had a stutter, which was made worse by all the teasing. He was hospitalized for depression and an attempted suicide."

Casey gasped, then glared at Jared. "He's an accountant now? Good."

Returning from lunch, Floyd drove past the window, and Casey pointed. "Oh goody. Another bully."

Arianna met Casey's gaze. Her pinched brows and scowl echoed Arianna's heart. With a sigh, Arianna pivoted and hurried to find Darius. She glanced back at Casey and heard. "So how would you like to support Arianna? May I suggest this design?"

CHAPTER FOURTEEN

"I LOVE IT!" Eva Adams cooed, as she spun in a circle, flaring her long skirt.

"You look like a fairy princess," Geoffrey, Eva's personal assistant said. He waved at Eva. "Let me take a few pictures of you to inspire Todd's hair design."

Arianna glanced over at Darius, who wore a smug expression. He caught her gaze and glanced at the ceiling, fluttering his eyelids, his version of the eye roll. He strutted between Geoffrey and Eva, waving his hand as if shooing a fly. "You don't want Todd, dear heart. It has to be Guillermo."

"You think?" Eva studied her dress. "It will break Todd's heart."

"And you know how he holds a grudge," Geoffrey added.

Eva nodded, shifting in front of the floor-length mirror. "Darius is right. Only Guillermo will do," she sighed.

"Right." Geoffrey woke his tablet and started tapping the screen. "I'll make the appointment. Be right back." He walked out of earshot, making the call.

Darius beamed. "How does it feel?"

Eva raised her arms, then rolled her shoulders. "It's a little tight. Heavy too."

Arianna tucked a stray blonde lock behind her ear. Eva caught Arianna's frowning reflection in the mirror.

"I love it, honestly, I do. I'll become accustomed to the wings' weight." Eva shrugged her shoulders several times, shaking her wings.

"They fold back like real dragonfly wings." Arianna moved Eva so she could see the profile in the mirror. A gentle tug had the wingtips together. "It sticks out behind you, but it streamlines your profile so you can get through doorways without shuffling sideways."

"Nice. I never would have thought about that." Eva shifted left and right, examining the iridescent material covering the wings. "The glittery veins are cool. How did you do it?"

Arianna grinned. Kyan had been her muse. "Metallic embroidery thread."

"You've outdone yourself, Arianna." Eva clapped, then spun again.

Arianna leaned against the wall, grateful she'd granted someone's happiness.

Her uncle's office door opened, and two frowning men in business suits exited, followed by Floyd waving his hands as he talked. The men paused as Floyd swept his arm in her direction. The younger man leered, making Arianna's skin crawl. After a few more moments of discussion, the men shook hands with Floyd.

She curled her finger beckoning Darius. Arianna whispered, "Who are those men?"

"I might have heard, but I'm not positive." Darius straightened his lavender bowtie. Arianna continued to stare at him until he fluttered his lids. "Fine. They're walking piggybanks."

Arianna covered her mouth and giggled. Darius snorted. "See if I tell you the rest." He crossed his arms and stuck his nose in the air.

She bit her lip, hiding her smile. "Come on. You're dying to tell me anyway," Arianna coerced, placing a hand on his arm.

"Fine." He covered her hand then tugged Arianna toward her office. "Ms. Adams, we'll return in a moment. Maud and

Diana will take care of you." He waved over his head, then shut the door behind him.

He cracked his knuckles, then leaned close and whispered. "They're your uncle's financial backers. Suits with money. They'll provide the funds for the expansion."

"Walking piggybanks." Arianna giggled again. "Wait. What expansion? We've already enlarged the store and added online shopping."

Darius shook his head, making his purple-framed glasses slip down his nose. "Lord have mercy on that uncle of yours." He pushed the glasses up. "He wants new locations."

"Oh." Arianna smiled. "Floyd always wanted to open a store across town."

Darius shook his head again. "Doesn't he ever tell you anything?"

Arianna bit her tongue, keeping the fact that she avoided Floyd to herself. She shrugged. "I'm usually the last on his list."

"He wants to move into other states' markets," Darius said.

"Move?" Arianna felt for her stool, then lowered herself. Her heart became lead. "I can't go." She couldn't leave Kyan. But what if Floyd built a bigger, better store in a new town in another state?

"Are you all right? You're as white as a ghost." Darius touched her forehead with the back of his hand. "Hmm."

The door burst open, and Floyd jumped into the room. "I've got news. We're expanding!" He shouted with joy. He put his hands on his hips, grinning like a superhero after catching a criminal. Floyd had left the door open and Eva could see him. "Well, what do you think?"

"Where?" Arianna squeaked.

"Atlanta and Nashville so far." Floyd glanced out the door, then blushed.

"Wow." Arianna hugged herself.

"I wish I could find places in Denver, Seattle, Chicago, and New York. I've put feelers out." He rubbed his chin. "My buddies, those men who just left, are going to help with the expenses. We are going big."

"What about this store?" Arianna asked, glancing toward Kyan hiding in the plant. "Are you going to keep it?"

Floyd laughed. "Sure, we are. It's the cheapest real estate. This is your domain and our home base. Though I plan to travel to get the ball rolling."

Ping. Floyd fished his phone out of his pocket and glanced at the screen. "I don't believe it. They've found the perfect location in New York."

"Uncle Ansen," Arianna said, twirling a strand of hair. "Those men are investors?"

Floyd invoked his used car salesmen smile. "Yes. And when they saw you, Newman and Theo were impressed. Because of you, they sealed the deal."

It felt as if the oxygen had gone from the room. Arianna grabbed the edge of her desk for support.

"Congratulations, Mr. Floyd. New York means you've arrived." Darius offered a thumbs up.

"It's a start." Floyd rubbed his palms together. "Arianna, you're the ticket to our riches and fame. We are going big time."

Arianna pasted on a grin similar to Floyd's. "Great."

"Oh, Darius. Get with Markus and draw up a schedule for the next year." Floyd scrolled through his phone.

"A year?" Darius glanced at Arianna. "When would you like it?"

"As soon as possible. Markus knows what I want." Floyd pivoted and retreated toward his office.

With a hand cocked on his hip, Darius frowned. "Markus. I don't trust that guy as far as I can throw him."

Arianna slunk onto her stool and slumped over the drafting table. "We have to plan designs for a year in advance?" She rubbed her forehead.

"I better start hunting for trend forecasts. I'll make a few calls. I know people." Darius straightened his bowtie.

"I suppose it's only fifty designs," Arianna whispered, glancing at Kyan.

"Markus isn't going to catch me off guard." Darius leaned against the table. "Listen, you've got this. With the holidays and seasons, you'll only have to fill in the other weeks."

Arianna straightened and began writing on a Post-it note. "December is basically Christmas or winter stuff."

"Right! See, you've got it. Halloween and Thanksgiving are fall. Valentine's, St. Patrick's Day, spring, then you have obscure holidays like national dog day." Darius pushed off the table. "I'm going to start a library of all the past designs."

Arianna nodded. "Once you've completed this, we can look through my sketchbook and see what months they'll fall within."

Darius grinned and pointed at her. "That's an excellent idea. We're going to need caffeine. I'll grab us something." He waved, hurrying out the door.

Arianna crossed her arms. The business was growing faster than she'd ever thought possible. Her designs continued to increase in popularity. It was a dream come true.

If her dreams were coming to fruition, then why was she not satisfied? She hugged herself tighter. Could her dreams change so swiftly?

Arianna loved drawing. She loved designing. And she finally had the support of her uncle, albeit it came with a price tag. She should be floating on cloud nine, but she felt empty.

Kyan landed on her open pad. "You will be busy this afternoon. Shall I see you tonight?"

The thought of staring into Kyan's caring blue eyes while talking mere inches apart made Arianna's heart race. She nodded, rubbing the warm spot in her chest. "I wouldn't miss it for the world."

"Which world?" Kyan laughed as he lifted off the paper.

Arianna giggled too. "Both." She walked to the glass door and opened it. The fresh air smelled earthy, and she longed to move her office outside. "I'll walk you to the tree."

"Thank you, my love. I am happy to have your companionship." He glided beside her the entire trek to the tree trunk. He saluted her. "Until tonight."

Arianna blew a kiss then skipped back to her office. She inhaled deeply before pulling open the door and returning to work.

CHAPTER FIFTEEN

I SHIFTED UNEASILY as I fumbled to fasten my trousers. The fabric was crisp and cool against my legs. Next came the white shirt. The neck was tighter than I liked, but for Arianna I'd wear a robe of snakes.

"Well?" Arianna called from above. She couldn't see me. I smiled and tucked in the shirt as she'd asked me. I wouldn't have minded trying the clothes while in the tree, but she had insisted I have two feet firmly on the ground. Besides the tightness around the collar, the clothing felt comfortable. I raised my hands over my head, then touched my toes.

"Patience, my love." I returned to the base of the tree, figuring the best way to climb it without damaging the clothing.

"Need a boost?" Jett asked. My brother leaned against a neighboring tree with his arms crossed. I hadn't heard him approach, and he wore clothes, both a sign he'd ridden from the palace.

"Where's your horse?"

"She's in the glen with the small spring." Jett pushed off the trunk and studied my attire. "Fancy."

Glancing down at what Arianna called dress pants, I nodded. "This is what the men of her world wear when they conduct business."

Jett arched a brow.

I picked up the jacket and slipped it on. "There are sometimes more pieces to it, but she needs to know if the measurements are correct."

"Is this what she's making you for the Harvest Moon?" Jett walked around me. He touched the elbow of the jacket.

"No." I glanced at the window between worlds. I had moved to where Arianna could now see me. "There are final touches needed on the tuxedo."

Arianna tucked a strand of hair behind her ear, then waved at Jett. He waved back.

"I can use your assistance," I said, pointing to the tree.

Jett braided his fingers, and I stepped into his hands. He hoisted me upward. I grabbed the branch, easily stepping onto it.

"What do you think, Arianna?" I asked.

Her silver-gray eyes narrowed as she studied the lines of the suit. "Put your arms at your side."

Leaning against the limb, I followed her instructions. She took notes as twilight fell behind her. She'd sat the backpack in front of her as a desk. The sketchpad balanced on top.

"Take the jacket off. I want to see how the shirt fits." Her sizzling gaze raked my torso. I enjoyed modeling for her. She continued, "Now step back a little so I can see your pants."

"Are the trousers the correct length?" The soft gasp Arianna made when I shook my bum had my dragon eager to please her.

"Perfect." She pulled her gaze from mine and jotted something on her pad. "I'll make a few adjustments but, mostly, everything looks good. What are you going to use the clothes for now?"

I glanced at the clothing from another world. They wouldn't survive the return trip and were mine to use as I chose. She had explained her world's ritual of selecting mates. "I will wear them on occasion to our nightly dates."

Arianna's eyes widened, her cheeks flushed as a delightful

smile blossomed on her lips. She tucked some hair behind her ear. "Okay. You look nice in the suit, but isn't it a little fancy for a tree?"

"I don't dress for the trees or the birds, but for you, my love." I longed to hold her in my arms.

"I, uh." Arianna blinked watery eyes. "I have shoes for you too. Let me get them for you to try." She held her notepad, shifting the backpack. The magic caught the pack's strap and sucked it in. My heart lurched when she shrieked. Dropping the pad, she lunged for the handle.

"Arianna, no!" I shouted. She gritted her teeth and pulled, fighting to keep the backpack in her world. The bag fizzled and glowed. Smoke rose from the middle with a putrid smell. "Let it go."

"But my work—"

"It will remain in my hands," I tried to reassure her.

Biting her lip, she nodded. She released the handle with a sigh. The steaming satchel landed in my arms.

"Inside the big pocket you'll find socks and shoes."

I opened the bag and found the items. The shoes slid on over the soft socks and fit comfortably. "These will do."

"You can wear them around inside to break them in. That way they won't hurt your feet." She peered at her hands. "Kyan?"

Her lip trembled and my heart ached. "Yes, my love?"

She continued to stare downward, her almost white hair contrasted by the darkening sky. "There is a sketchpad in my backpack that's private. No one has ever seen any of those drawings, not even Darius."

"Arianna," I breathed. She glanced up, and her breath caught. "It would give me great pleasure if I could view your work, but should you choose it to remain private, my dragon can reduce it to ash."

"Don't burn it." She swallowed but shook her head. "You may look at them, but make sure you are alone."

"You have my word," I vowed. I glanced down to find my

brother's upturned face pondering the bag. Jett's gaze panned the item, then he met my eyes. He raised his brows, and I frowned.

"Kyan?" Arianna leaned forward, her hair cascading over her shoulders. Her fingers traced the lines of bark on the branch. "It's not fashion drawings."

"I will enjoy your work because it is a part of you." I studied her lips as they bowed downward. Her hair rippled as she shook her head. "Your art expresses facets of your soul."

Wide-eyed, her head shot up and her gaze caught mine. Those lovely silver eyes sparkled with the reflected portal glow. The silence expanded, but it only drew my heart closer to Arianna. Both worlds faded, until I only saw, smelled, and heard my mate.

"You're going to break the magic window staring like that," Jett hollered from below me. I stomped the branch, shaking debris onto Jett.

Arianna's eyes crinkled as a smile broke out. She covered her mouth and giggled. The sound was glorious, like chimes on a windy day. My irritation at my brother faded, and I joined her laughing.

Our conversation turned to the Harvest Moon ball. Arianna asked questions about the dresses, music, food, and people. I tried to answer, but since I was obligated to attend I'd never paid much attention to the details. "Why don't you come see for yourself as my date?"

Jett snorted. I could imagine his bulging wide eyes and open mouth.

"Oh." Arianna's eyelids fluttered and her cheeks flushed. "That's kind of you, but…" She glanced toward the store and sighed. "I wish I could."

"There you go, wishing when I am here and can't grant your wishes." I tugged on the collar, feeling heat clog my throat.

"I would love to go with you, Kyan, but I wouldn't be

visiting Ellehcor, I'd have to stay forever. Remember? I can't return through the portal." She rubbed her palms on her thighs.

"I remember." I attempted to keep my tone even. "Come with me."

Arianna tilted her head, studying me anew. "What would happen to me after the dance? Where would I stay? What would I do? I'd have nowhere to live." She stared past me.

"I would take care to provide for you." With my hand over my heart, I swore this. "Think on it, Arianna. The decision is yours to make."

Stars winked in the sky between the leaves behind Arianna. She tried to hide a yawn. "I better go before I fall asleep and tumble out of the tree."

We said our farewells, and I stood at the portal until I could no longer hear her footfalls. I removed the shoes and socks, returning them to the backpack, then jumped to the forest floor.

Jett had disappeared, leaving me to my thoughts. I sat in a patch of sunny grass and searched the backpack for Arianna's sketchpad. The first pencil drawing was a mirror reflection of my face. Except for the coloring, her talent was such I could have thought myself a twin. The next few pages were various body parts, my hands, shoulder, profile, and my backside.

I flipped the page and gasped. Arianna and I stood side by side holding hands and gazing into each other's eyes. In the next, my hands plunged into her silky hair as I pulled her close. I remained frozen, my lips a mere breath from hers. Just as the portal separated us now. Would I ever find out the softness of her lips?

I found it hard to breathe, but I continued turning the pages. There were several of me posing in the tuxedo she was creating for me. She drew me with such realism, each line a touch of love. My heart raced as I realized my mate cared for me as I cared for her.

I turned the page. There before me I had proof. My mate

and I stood in our finery, facing each other. I recognized the tuxedo, but I'd never seen Arianna's dress. Her attention to details, the texture, shadows, and our expressions of longing had me wishing this was our memory.

CHAPTER SIXTEEN

ARIANNA RUSHED INTO Floyd's office, meeting Darius and Markus gathered around Floyd's desk. She opened her laptop, ready to take notes. Darius took a seat next to her.

"Just a moment," Markus said. He tapped his laptop's keypad, then glanced up at the flat screen TV on the wall. "Almost got it."

Darius leaned close to Arianna. "This will be interesting. Why did they schedule the meeting in Atlanta?"

"The investors and Uncle Ansen's schedule's coincided while he was there. I think we were an oversight." Arianna nervously laughed.

"Mr. Floyd wants me to take notes." Markus smiled when the screen winked on.

"Couldn't you just record it?" Darius asked.

The view changed to a large room with a conference table. Men gathered around. There was no audio, but they were obviously talking. At least, Floyd was waving his hands, bloviating. The poor sap across the table hunched over his notepad, writing frantically.

The curser slid over the screen, and Markus clicked a button. Floyd's commandeering voice boomed over the TV speakers. Markus lowered the volume. "We're muted."

"I recognize a few of the men," Arianna said. The two

businessmen who'd visited the store sat at the table. The younger man noticed they had joined the meeting, and Floyd quieted.

Arianna tried to remain focused on the figures, timetables, and ideas spouted, but her mind wandered toward her work for Kyan's mother's dress and Kyan's offer. As a child, she'd dreamed of being a princess. With Kyan it was possible... wasn't it? She shook her head.

The smarmy younger business man must have been watching her. "Arianna?"

She shivered, and Darius patted her hand. "Yes? I'm here."

"Hello, I'm Theo Masters. It's good of you to join us," he offered. "Do you have your designs for the year?"

Arianna tried to keep her face neutral and kept from rolling her eyes, although Darius fluttered his lids. They'd only received Floyd's mandate earlier that week. "Of course," she replied.

"What? Really?" Theo glanced at Floyd.

"No. Not really. I think I need slightly longer than a few days. But thanks for thinking I work that fast." She saluted the screen.

The gray-haired Newman laughed. Even Floyd cracked a grin.

"Actually, Arianna has designs through the end of this calendar year. When does the fiscal year begin? Or are we staying with the calendar year?" Darius asked.

The men at the table all started talking at once. "I could hug you," Arianna whispered to Darius.

She heard Theo mumble something tongue in cheek about cockroach fashion designs coinciding with hockey season.

"Cockroaches? O.M.G. It's dragonflies." Darius whipped his hand around in the air.

Arianna appreciated Darius' affronted attitude, but her squirrel brain had flashed into design mode. She opened a program on her laptop and began searching for a background. A few minutes later she had a concept she liked.

Darius leaned close, watching her work.

Newman noticed her working and nudged Floyd. "Arianna," Floyd's irritated tone made her suck in a breath. She bit her lip. "Pay attention."

"Yes, Uncle." Arianna sighed. She began to close her laptop, but Darius stopped her.

"Mr. Floyd, I think you should see what Arianna has just designed." Darius turned the laptop around.

"Here. Let me have it." Markus took the laptop and plugged it into the call. He shared Arianna's screen.

"What is this?" Floyd asked, still sounding annoyed.

A stylized cockroach danced over the yellow and black symbol for hazardous waste. "Something Mr. Masters said spurred the idea. It's a concept drawing."

"Something for the new men's line?" Darius asked with an enormous grin.

"Yes!" Arianna smiled at him.

"That's brilliant," Theo said. "I inspired it, huh?" He leaned backward. His ego seeming to inflate his chest. "Maybe you can return the favor and inspire me." He wiggled his eyebrows, and most of the men laughed.

A wave of nausea rolled over Arianna. She sought her uncle's gaze. Floyd shifted uneasily, and she clutched her stomach. She understood Floyd was at the mercy of his investors, and it couldn't bode well for her.

"I'll be in your neck of the woods the beginning of November." Theo said, glancing up from his calendar. "How does that work for you, Arianna?"

Stunned to silence, she glanced at Darius for help. A blue blur whizzed by. Markus squealed and jumped up.

"What's going on there?" Newman asked.

"Look!" Darius pointed to their live screen on the TV. Kyan's dragonfly body blocked their camera. His dark shadow separated Arianna from Theo's lecherous gaze.

Markus raised a book over his head. "I'll take care of it."

Arianna hopped up, toppling her chair. "No. I'll get him."

She cupped her hands, and Kyan landed. "You might have damaged the computer," she said over her shoulder to Markus.

Darius righted her chair, and Arianna returned to her seat. Hands in her lap, she kept Kyan out of sight. "Uncle Ansen, what do you think of a shirt specifically for each location?"

"Like that restaurant?" Darius asked.

Arianna nodded and added, "Except it wouldn't have the same logo with different locations. I'd create a design to relate to that state. The customer could only buy it on site."

"Palm trees for Florida, peaches for Georgia, that kind of thing?" Floyd asked, rubbing his chin. "The Bean in Chicago."

"Don't worry. We'll get that space at a discount," the man on Theo's right said.

"I wish it was that easy," Floyd replied.

The man glanced at his phone. "Oh! It went through. We have Chicago."

Arianna peered downward. Kyan tilted his head. His little leg brushed her thumb.

"Each store is a destination." Newman smiled. "You have a keen mind for business, Arianna." The men murmured excitedly to one another.

"I think we're done with your portion, Arianna. We'll let you get back to work. Thanks for joining us." Floyd nodded then continued, "Markus stay on the line."

"Okay. Back to work." Darius picked up Arianna's laptop and followed her to the office. "Maud needs me. I'll be back in a moment."

Arianna nodded as he left. She opened her hands next to the potted plant, and Kyan ambled onto a leaf. "What were you thinking?" she scolded. "Markus could have squished you."

"I could not abide that man's behavior toward you." Kyan's wings fluttered. "He is not honorable."

She sighed and scrubbed her face. Taking a seat on the stool, she slumped over the desk. "I know. Theo gives me the willies."

Kyan stomped around in a circle. "Where are these willies he gave to you?"

Arianna giggled. "Oh, Kyan. I needed that laugh, thank you."

He tipped his head. "Anything for you, my love."

"Willies are a bad feeling. When he looks at me, I feel gross." She sighed and flipped open a notebook to an empty page. A dark creature came to mind. She sketched thick, heavy-handed lines. "Anyway, I may not be here when he comes to the store."

"Where will you be?" Darius said, entering with a large mug of coffee. He handed it to Arianna.

She slipped on the ambrosia and hummed. "You are awesome."

"Tell me something I don't already know, like where you are planning to go." He folded his arms over his chest and tapped his foot.

Arianna returned to work on her drawing. "Have I told you I've been invited to a ball?"

"The royal ball? Shut up." Darius pulled the other stool close. "Girl, you better spill the deets."

Arianna added curving horns to the creature's head. She pushed the finished work toward Darius. He glanced at it and snickered. "I know who *inspired* this. What do you want to call it?"

"Diablo." Arianna stretched, twisting side to side.

"Now about this invitation…?" Darius pushed his purple glasses up the bridge of his nose. "I'm not letting you alone until you tell me about this dreamy prince you're madly in love with."

Arianna's face flashed hot, and she glanced away from the planter where Kyan hid. "He asked me to the dance, that's all."

"It is not and you know it." Darius tapped his chin. "What are you going to wear?"

"I haven't agreed to go." Arianna picked at a nail.

"What?" Darius touched her hand. "Are you crazy? It's a once in a lifetime chance."

Arianna bit her lip. Her heart soared at the thought of spending the evening twirling about the dance floor in Kyan's muscular arms. She held her breath.

"It's because he's a prince and you're not royalty, isn't it?" Darius patted her hand. "You are an up-and-coming fashion star, Arianna. If he can't accept you for who you are then—"

"He's not like that. He's noble, respectful, and kind." Arianna held the coffee under her nose and inhaled. Warmth radiated inside. She loved the scent of coffee. Did they have coffee in Ellehcor?

"I think you should wear that," Darius pointed to one of the framed dresses.

"I'd love to, but we don't have enough time to make it."

Darius cracked his knuckles. "Watch me work." He hopped off the stool. "Maud!" He dashed out of the office. A minute later, Darius took the picture off the wall. Maud listened as Darius ordered Arianna to describe her dream dress.

"It has to match the prince's tux," Darius declared.

"The skirt layers should be silver. The bodice: white." Arianna pointed to the angled waist where a butterfly-shaped bow hung on the right hip. "I don't want a butterfly. I'd like a dragonfly."

"This looks like a square neckline." Maud furrowed her brows. "The straps are wider. Maybe an inch. I prefer straps. You'll look like a princess in this."

"That's the point." Darius grinned, and Maud nodded, agreeing with him. "Maybe you can hook the prince and reel him in."

Arianna's mouth flopped open like a fish. Even while her friends played matchmaker, Arianna's thoughts churned almost as much as her stomach.

CHAPTER SEVENTEEN

"BE CAREFUL," ARIANNA fretted as Kyan pulled the large dress bag through the shimmering portal. She bit her lip as the last of it slipped into his world. The magic barrier seemed to crackle, or it could have been her nerves. "How is it?"

Kyan lifted the thin plastic covering. "The gown looks fine."

She blew out a sigh and slumped over the next dress bag containing his tuxedo. Shirtless, Kyan whistled. Jett in dragon form appeared and offered an upturned claw. Kyan hung the hanger on the claw.

"This is heavier than I thought it would be," Jett said, narrowing his eyes.

Kyan faced Arianna once more. "Next."

The metal hook broke the barrier first, tugging the rest in. Kyan caught his suit and added it to Jett's other claw. "Take these home. I'm sure Mother will want her gown immediately."

"I hope it fits fine," Arianna said.

"Do not worry, my love. You took care to make it perfect. And even if it needs minor adjustments, there are plenty of seamstresses talented enough in my world." Kyan rubbed his arm, and Arianna realized she'd been staring at his chest.

"Do you like the sweatpants?" Arianna asked.

"I do," Jett said. "My brother boasts of your gift, and I must agree they are soft and flexible."

Kyan laughed. "It's true. He tried to wear mine today before we left the palace."

"I'm glad you like them." Arianna reached for another bag hanging on a stubby branch. "I have something for you."

The portal slurped the bag, and Kyan caught it by one handle. Some items tumbled toward the ground.

"This is generous of you." He searched the bag, pulling out two more pairs of gray sweatpants, plain white cotton T-shirts and packages of socks.

"I don't know Jett's size, but if those fit I can buy more." Arianna said, studying the dragon's black scales. "I have something for your mom too."

Kyan opened his mouth to protest, but Arianna hurried on. "It's nothing much. Just a perfume fragrance my mom loved. Your mother may have a more sensitive nose than mine did. Anyway, she doesn't have to wear it."

"It was very kind to consider her," Jett said. He shifted the garment bags to one side. "I must be off. It was good to see you, Arianna. Take care." He unfurled his wings. With one thrust, he launched into the sky, leaving Kyan alone.

Arianna studied the golden box. It wasn't cheap perfume, but it had been her mother's favorite. The scent reminded Arianna of happier times. She sighed and presented it to the portal's mouth. The box arrived unfettered, and Kyan put it into the shopping bag with his clothes.

"She will appreciate your kindness." Kyan stepped close to the portal. The magical glow reflected in his piercing blue eyes. "I'm reluctant to leave you, but I am required to assist Jett and my brothers in preparing for our guests' arrival."

"I know. Enjoy your family time. I have to work, Darius is probably wondering where I am." Arianna blew Kyan a kiss. "I'll see you later."

"That is a promise." With a wave, he dropped out of the tree. A moment later, a blue dragon winked at her, then took to the sky. His serpentine neck, broad-winged shoulders, and long tail always left her in awe. A dragon performing a barrel roll for her pleasure, didn't leave her breathless and weak-kneed as much as Kyan's longing gaze upon her.

Arianna glanced at her watch, then down at a pile of boxes. She listened to both world's birdsong. Eerily similar, but slightly different. She climbed down and propped the step stool to reach the portal. Hoisting a box, she ascended the steps. Balancing, she placed the package at the glowing opening. Giving it a nudge, the magic pulled it in with a flash and a pop.

"That worked well. Only twelve more." Arianna gathered her hair into a ponytail. She continued until all boxes had entered Kyan's world.

"Arianna," a deep voice grumbled.

She jumped, startled by the undeniable rumble of a dragon. She clambered up to the branch once more. "Kyan?" An amber eye filled the window. Black scales reflected the pale glow. "Jett."

"I see you've been busy." He chuckled, shaking the trees in both worlds.

"Thank you for storing the stuff."

"And what will you tell Kyan?" Jett asked. A clear lid blinked.

"Nothing for now. And if you'd like a few pairs of sweatpants, then you'll do the same." She crossed her arms, staring him in the eye.

"As you wish. Is there any more today?" Jett asked, tilting his head as if hearing a noise.

"Nope. Not today. I've got to go." With a wave, she headed toward the back of the strip mall. A design idea flitted through her consciousness, and she picked up her gait.

As Arianna reached the back door, it swung open. Casey bounded out, Darius following. "There you are. You've got to see what's on the TV."

"Eva Adams?" Arianna asked, letting them tug her inside. They gathered in the store. Several customers shopped. The midday news reported the weather forecast. "It's going to rain this weekend?"

"Just wait. It's coming up," Casey said with hands on her hips and a pouty face.

"Did you teach her that?" Arianna asked Darius, pointing to Casey.

"No siree, she's got her own talents." Darius laughed.

"In other news: local businessman Ansen Floyd, owner of Floyd's Apparel and Embroidery, is in talks to acquire Canadian clothier Lauren Cline. Floyd's Apparel and Embroidery has opened stores in Atlanta, Chicago, and New York City, to name a few places. The company's recent success is due in part to the artistic talent of Arianna Travers. Travers, Floyd's niece, designs graphics for the store's clothing line: Dragonfly Wishes. Her weekly designs have gone viral."

A picture of Eva Adams modeling one of Arianna's early dragonfly drawings appeared on the screen, then transitioned to a shot of the outside of the store.

"Travers also offers personal custom works." The TV cut to an interview with Eva in the gown Arianna had designed.

"Look how beautiful Eva is," Darius whispered.

"Arianna's creations are a dream come true. Look at this craftsmanship. Everyone on her team was fabulous to work with. I highly recommend trying them for your special events," Eva gushed.

A view of the smiling anchorwoman replaced Eva. "Floyd's Apparel and Embroidery has something for everyone. Visit the store on Oakmount Avenue or their website to find the design of the week."

"Wow." Arianna leaned against a T-stand.

"They should have shown a picture of you," Casey said, shaking her head. She retreated behind the counter to ring up a couple of shoppers.

"I'm glad they didn't," Arianna mumbled.

"Are you her?" A college-aged girl asked Casey, gesturing to the T-shirt of the week she was purchasing.

"She is." Casey thumbed over her shoulder toward Arianna.

"Ms. Travers, can you sign my shirt?" the girl pleaded. Her bright white teeth shone in the florescent light.

"Mine too," her red-headed friend said, waving a shirt.

"Sure. Let me find something to write with." Arianna turned but smacked into Darius' hand holding a black permanent marker. "Thanks."

"I got your back." He grinned and motioned for the groupies to move to a vacant counter area. "Come over here, ladies. Who's first?" He smoothed out the shirt then slid a folding board inside.

Arianna signed the shirts for the friends, then Casey had her hang around for an hour to accommodate other customers. Arianna's feet ached when she left the store to hide in her office.

Darius handed her a coffee. "I hope this merger goes through." He sipped his own beverage.

"I didn't know a thing about it. Why do you want the merger?" She sat on her stool, holding her mug.

"Well, let's just say we are going international." Darius gazed dreamily at nothing. "It's big time. Lauren Cline has locations worldwide." He ticked them off on his fingers. "London, Sydney, Stockholm, Bern, Paris, Buenos Aires, Rio de Janeiro, Tel Aviv…"

Darius continued to drone on, but Arianna tuned him out. Her mind drifted like a dragonfly on the wind. She opened a sketchbook and started doodling. First trees and falling leaves, then individual oak, maple, and sycamore leaves. Stylized and realistic. A small blue dragon whelp peeking from under a pile of leaf litter.

Would Kyan's kids be blue dragons? Could baby dragons breathe fire? That would be bad for breastfeeding. She cringed and shook her head. Darius had gone, and she discovered several pages of designs.

Tink. Tink. Something tapped on the glass door. Kyan hovered near the handle. She opened the door, and he buzzed in. He landed on her coffee mug handle. "My mother shouted for joy when she tried on the gown. She loved it."

"I'm glad." Arianna sat and leaned over him. His iridescent body shimmered a mesmerizing shade of blue. He hopped into the air, landing on her nose. "Oh," she squeaked.

"Mother was touched at your thoughtfulness about the perfume and, yes, she likes the scent. My old governess was helping Mother with the fitting and enjoyed the scent to the point of tears. She claimed nostalgia for her emotions." He fluttered to the notepad.

"Would you like me to buy a bottle for your governess? It's not a big deal." Arianna woke her laptop and typed in the brand's name.

"That is kind of you, but unnecessary." Kyan waved his hand.

"Done." She giggled when he tilted his head. "You've got to be faster."

He chuckled, then folded his front two arms. "Tell me of your day. Did you miss me as I have missed you?"

"Every minute." Dragonflies launched in her stomach, and she couldn't squelch her smile. "Wait until you hear what happened. They mentioned the shop on the TV today." She dove into a detailed story, recalling the news and the autograph aftermath.

"The people appreciate your talent, my love. The store is prospering." He walked onto Arianna's finger.

A loud knock, then her door burst open. Floyd stomped in with a swagger. "You saw the report?"

"Yes, Uncle. It's… wow." Arianna couldn't string together the words.

"The merger meeting is night." Floyd nodded, rubbing his balding crown. His gaze zeroed in on Kyan. Arianna stiffened and held her breath. "The wish granting bug. No wonder your designs went viral. You had help."

Arianna gasped. Kyan flew to her shoulder and pointed at Floyd. "She needs no magical assistance. Each drawing comes from the magic within Arianna."

Floyd grabbed Arianna's arm, jerking her and launching Kyan into the air. He hovered over her desk, out of Floyd's reach.

"You've granted her wishes," the Overlord growled. His dewy face reddened.

"I have not." Kyan flew in a Z shape. "She has not—"

"Liar." He yelled, spittle spraying the desk. "It doesn't matter. I wish the merger is a success."

"Are you certain you wish this?" Kyan asked, hovering in place.

"Duh. The merger means more money. More business. More prestige. Something a bug wouldn't understand." Floyd threw a disgusted look at Kyan, then pointed at Arianna. "What's good for the store is good for you. Be here tomorrow to learn your fate."

CHAPTER EIGHTEEN

ARIANNA HOISTED A rolling bag out of her car. Approaching the store, she inspected the bright words painted on the window. Casey's idea was genius. It counted down the days until the new design became available. Arianna rolled the suitcase up the handicap ramp, then along the sidewalk. She rounded the corner toward the backside. A green trash truck emptied the dumpster with an earsplitting boom.

She fished her key out of her hefty purse, an inadequate replacement for her backpack. As she twisted the key, she gazed longingly at the forest. She inhaled a deep breath, then hurried inside.

She flipped on the light and set her bags in the corner. Arianna glanced at the framed art on the wall and giggled. She modeled her design with a blue skirt and white blouse. Today she even had worn heels.

Arianna walked into the showroom and nodded at John, who counted the till. He waved a fist full of money. Casey wiped down the window, removing the three.

"Hey there," Arianna said.

Startled, Casey dropped a paper towel wad. "Geesh. Don't do that, I've only got one heart." Her eyes darted toward the door connecting the offices to the store. "How are you?"

"Translation: why are you here?" Arianna laughed. "I just

wanted to tell you this is a brilliant idea." She gestured to the window. "I know my uncle wouldn't ever tell you."

"Thank you. No, I haven't heard from the Overlord." Casey sprayed the glass with cleaner, then wiped the colored streaks. "It takes a little to paint the numbers backwards, but I have a printout I use."

"Cheater." Arianna giggled. Casey dropped her paper towel again. "I'm kidding. Better you than me."

"Uh huh. I thought so." Casey faced Arianna, shifting her feet. "I've heard stuff."

Arianna inhaled. Exhaling slowly, she asked, "What stuff? The merger?"

"No. Well, yeah, that too, but no. You're in love with some royal dude and are going to leave to attend a fall ball?" Casey cocked her hip with her hand on it.

"I—"

"How did you not tell me about this? Seriously?" Casey pinched her features, mimicking her uncle's confounded expression.

Arianna held her hands in surrender. "I can explain, sorta." She stepped closer and gazed out the window. "I didn't mean it to happen, but it just did." She shrugged, turning toward her friend.

"Love is like that. Sometimes it's a gradual thing and sometimes… Bam!" Casey slapped her hands together. "It hits you like a ton of bricks."

Arianna nodded, twirling a strand of hair. "He asked me to the dance, but I haven't decided if I want to go."

"But—"

Arianna held up her hand. "It's not that simple, Casey. If I go, I'm never coming back. Ever."

"Never ever? Oh, wow. He proposed too?" Casey gaped, her hands on her cheeks. "Wowzers."

"Arianna," Darius called, motioning for her. "You better come listen to this. Floyd isn't happy with the merger, and I keep hearing your name."

Arianna threw an apologetic glance toward Casey, then hurried to meet Darius. A look over her shoulder confirmed Casey followed her.

"This can't be," Floyd shouted. He muttered curses between bursts. Another man attempted to soothe her uncle; however, it only inflamed him. "It's not a merger but a takeover!"

Arianna inched toward the office door and peered between the door crack. Floyd paced by his desk. The other man she recognized as her uncle's attorney friend, Wilson Thomas.

"I wish you had let me read the documents before signing them," Wilson said, shifting through a pile of papers.

"Time was of the essence. There was a deadline." Floyd rubbed his balding forehead.

Wilson remained silent as he scanned the document. Arianna glanced at Darius, Casey, Maud, Markus, and Diana, who couldn't help overhearing Floyd's ranting. Maud wrung her hands, and Diana chewed her lip.

Arianna stepped away from the door and pointed to Markus and Darius. "We need coffee and pastries ASAP. You know that little bakery that Uncle Ansen loves?"

"Mighty Muffin? Sure," Markus replied.

"Go and get a couple dozen donuts or whatever. Get coffee for us all too. Darius, I have cash in my purse." The men nodded and after they'd left Arianna said to Maud and Diana, "Is my dress done? Hang it in my office, then get back to work. You too, Casey. You shouldn't leave John by himself. I'll figure out what's going on. I'm sure it's just some oversight."

The noise level in the office ebbed. Arianna stood alone in the hallway, missing Kyan's familiar presence. Fear held her outside Floyd's office, peeking in. She wasn't fond of eavesdropping, but she couldn't risk triggering Floyd's volatile temper.

"It doesn't look good." Wilson removed his readers and rubbed his eyes.

"This can't be legal." Floyd sat elbows on the desk, head in his hands. "This isn't anything like they said."

"It's legal, all right. You will have a hard time getting out of this deal." Wilson straightened and stacked the papers. "You should have read the details before signing."

Floyd balled his fist and slammed it on the desk. "They needed it fast. I skimmed the first few, then just…" He growled. "This is fraud."

Wilson put his glasses back on and shifted the papers. Glancing at the top paper, he said, "Lauren Cline is the parent company. You've sold Floyd's Apparel and Embroidery. The sum is paltry. And that's not the worst part."

"I know." Floyd uttered. "I still owe Theo Masters and Newman Bolduc money. And the stores—"

"Belong to Lauren Cline now. You can't use the stores as collateral. Do you have any savings?" Wilson asked.

"Everything I earned I put into the expansion." Floyd huffed. "Arianna could—"

"Arianna belongs to Lauren Cline too," Wilson said.

She gasped. *How in the world?* Thoughts of a leering Theo Masters made her shiver. Arianna shoved open the door. "What have you done, Uncle Ansen?"

Wilson stood as she entered the office. Floyd's mouth opened and closed like a fish.

"It's bad," Wilson said. "He's lost the business, and he's lost you. And on top of that, his investors are calling their loan due."

"Lost?" Arianna crossed her arms. She glared at the Overlord.

"You now work for Lauren Cline. You have an exclusivity contract with them. All your future art, as well as previous designs, are theirs. They've bought the rights. All concepts are their intellectual property." Wilson tugged on his collar.

Overwhelmed, Arianna felt behind for the chair next to Wilson's. Her knees gave out, and she dropped into the seat. A suppressive darkness settled over her. She gulped air. All her work gone? She covered her face and shook her head.

"There's more," Floyd whispered.

Arianna held her breath.

"You are supposed to move to their headquarters in Toronto. Lauren Cline's design hub is there." Floyd rubbed his chin.

"I never agreed to this. They can't make me move." Arianna hugged herself. She wouldn't leave Kyan.

"You were the attraction. Arianna, because of you they wanted Floyd's Apparel and Embroidery." Floyd stood and began pacing. "I don't know how I'm going to pay Theo and Newman back. The house is already mortgaged, and my car isn't worth anything."

Fire pooled in Arianna's gut, building until it consumed her. She vaulted out of her seat. "You used me as a negotiating prize, then sold me to the highest bidder. How dare you. And now you're worried about yourself. Pathetic." She glared at Floyd, whom she'd stunned into silence.

Arianna turned to leave, but paused at the door when Floyd asked, "Can't you wish it all back?"

"Kyan isn't here. He warned you about this deal, but you didn't listen. And, no thanks to you, I'm paying the price." An idea, a glint of light penetrated her darkness. "I quit."

"Lauren Cline still owns your backlog. You can't design for anyone else for five years, and anything you draw belongs to them in that time period." Floyd leaned against his desk, appearing aged ten years.

Her only family in this world had selfishly sold her out. Kyan had warned them. She walked like a zombie to her office and shut the door. Quiet pervaded the room, but her mind would not still.

In a sudden flurry, she rushed around, pulling everything out and stowing what she could in her purse. Careful not to mar the frames, she took the pictures off the wall. No one would have her designs.

Darius poked his head in. His mouth made a perfect O as he scanned the mess. "Coffee?" he asked, offering a paper cup as temptation.

"Thank you," she replied, taking the offered java. "As you can see, I'm leaving. He sold me out, Darius. My uncle." Tears pooled, but she shook her head, releasing Floyd's last hold over her.

"Wait a sec," Darius said, shoving his index finger into the air. "I'll be back." A moment later, Darius returned with Casey. They both carried an armload of shopping bags.

"We're here to help," Casey said with a sniffle. Arianna pulled her into a hug.

"Thank you." They packed her items in silence. When her desk and drawers were empty, the reality of her decision had the dragonflies in her stomach jousting.

Maud knocked on the door. "There's a Mr. Masters here to see Arianna." She swallowed as she panned the room.

"I'll run interference," Darius said, turning to Casey. "Get her out of here." He took Arianna's hands in his and squeezed. "You are talented, chic, and kind. Go to your prince and make lots of babies." He hauled her into a fierce hug.

Arianna patted his back. "I'm going to miss you." She let him go. Darius blew a kiss as he slipped from the room.

Casey rubbed her hands together. "How many bags can you carry?"

"As many as possible. We aren't going very far." Arianna picked up three in each hand.

Casey mimicked Arianna, then pushed open the back door with her bum and held it for Arianna. Casey followed her into the forest behind the strip mall.

"Are you really leaving us?" Casey asked, glancing at her shoes.

Arianna linked elbows with Casey as they doubled back to the office. A dragonfly flitted across their path, and Arianna's breath hitched. The body was pale chartreuse, not brilliant blue. They retrieved the last of the items, including the rolling suitcase and dress bag.

In the glen, Casey scanned the woods. "Is he meeting you

here?"

"It's hard to understand, but I'm leaving this world." Arianna set the step stool against the tree. "Will you hand me that bag?" She pointed to a shopping bag full of her art supplies.

Casey handed her bag after bag. "I get taking off, but is this guy worth it?"

"Yes," Arianna breathed, a wide smile filling her face. She shoved another item through the portal.

"Why are you stuffing the hole in that tree?" Casey asked, standing on her tiptoes.

"It's not just a hole. It's a window to another world." Arianna stepped down. "See for yourself."

Casey ascended the steps. "What the...?" she gasped. "It's so bright."

"Keep staring."

"Oh, there are trees and a purple bird. Is that a... black dragon? Holy smokes!" Casey jumped back, missing the step. Arianna caught her, but they both tumbled to the ground. Eyes closed, Casey covered her heart. Her rapid breathing reassured Arianna that she hadn't had a heart attack.

Arianna brushed off her skirt. One item remained. She hoisted the suitcase, but it proved tricky to keep balanced. Casey climbed up next to her and helped to steady it. The corner caught and the magic sucked it in, jerking it out of the women's hands. With a flash and a pop, it disappeared.

"Whoa." Casey rubbed her eyes.

"My turn." Arianna hugged her friend. "I'll miss you."

"I'll miss you too. Do you think your phone will work over there?" Casey tilted her head.

Arianna giggled. "Maybe near the tree. We can try it." Casey helped Arianna as she mounted the branch sidesaddle. She glanced into the portal, knowing Jett was there but hoping Kyan would be there too. The woods appeared empty except for the strange violet bird watching from another tree. Shadows on the forest floor caught her attention. Kyan came into view, and she sighed.

"There he is," Arianna said to Casey, who strained on her tippy toes. "Kyan," Arianna breathed.

"I can't see." Casey climbed onto the branch behind Arianna. Casey peered around Arianna and hummed. "I can totally see why you spend time in the woods." Casey giggled, poking Arianna in the side.

Jett lifted Kyan, and Arianna heard Casey gasp. Thankfully, Kyan had worn clothes, his princely attire of a linen shirt, dark pants, and polished boots.

"My love," Kyan greeted, meeting her eyes.

"This is my friend, Casey. She's put up with my uncle too."

"Greetings, Casey. Thank you for supporting Arianna." Kyan nodded. "Arianna…"

"Do you still want me to come?" Arianna whispered around the emotion clogging her throat.

Casey clamped Arianna around the waist. "Wait. Kyan, do you promise to care for and love Arianna? I don't want her to travel there and you get sick of her and feed her to your big black pet."

Arianna giggled. "That's Jett, Kyan's brother. Kyan is a blue dragon," Arianna informed Casey.

"I promise I'll cherish Arianna always." Kyan winked at Arianna, making the dragonflies take flight again.

Jett stuck his long neck around Kyan. A tendril of smoke escaped from his nostrils. "I wouldn't eat Arianna."

Casey hid behind Arianna. "He looks hungry." Kyan and Arianna chuckled. Jett snorted and disappeared, muttering about a Casey-dilla.

"Are you ready?" Kyan asked, stretching his arms for her.

Arianna smiled. "More than ready." She reached for the opening. Her finger touched the shimmering magic, shooting warm tingles up her arm. Surrounded by light, what started as a sensation of floating turned into turbulence. Spurted out, then falling, she flailed her arms. Kyan snagged her out of the air, cradling her.

Her head on his broad chest, she felt his strong heart beating. His woodsy scent tantalized her senses as she snuggled against him.

"Arianna," Casey studied her from the other side. "Are you okay?"

Safe in her dragon shifter's arms, Arianna nodded. "I am now."

EPILOGUE

I HELD MY mate's hand as we gazed out over the Harvest Moon attendees. The tuxedo she'd made for me was as unique as our love story. I caressed her cheek, and she rewarded me with a pretty pink blush.

Mother and Father stood regally as they approached the balcony's center. The crowd hushed as the fanfare played. All gazed upon the King and Queen.

I glanced over at my brothers Jett, Salokin, Cordovian, and my sisters, Zaffrie and Nyanza, wondering where the rest of my brothers hid. Only fourteen-year-old Zaffrie wore a deep blue gown, designed by Arianna. Three years older, Nyanza had likewise requested a gown. Her pale complexion and dark waves, accented by the pale yellow dress, would draw many suitors.

Pillars of tan marble with veins of russet gleamed in the light. The oversized windows exposed the sun setting over the garden. A brisk breeze blew through open glass doors.

Mother lifted her hand as she stepped forward. Her dress shimmered as if someone had painted it with pearls. "Esteemed family and guests, welcome to Ellehcor's one hundred and forty-first Harvest Moon ball."

The crowd cheered and clapped. Several raised glasses.

"Today is a celebration. We gather to partake in the harvest's bounty. Ellehcor's record reaping is a cause for joy." The queen gazed at her countrymen with affection.

My father tenderly touched Mother's hand and smiled at her. His thinly woven crown glinted in the sunlight. Waitstaff holding silver trays meandered through the hall, offering flutes of sparkling wine to the audience.

"We have an announcement," the king declared. "Our third-born Kyan has found a mate."

Arianna and I stepped forward, stopping beside Mother. We peered over the balcony at the eager faces. Arianna swallowed as she scanned the gathering. I squeezed her hand, and she gazed at me with those sparkling silver eyes. "You are glowing, my love," I uttered only for her.

She blushed, and with a smirk, she replied, "I must be a dragon."

"To Kyan!" someone yelled from below. I searched and found my next younger brother Falun, raising a glass. The crowd chuckled.

I pointed to Falun. "Your turn is coming." Again the assembly laughed.

"Ellehcor, I present Kyan's mate, Arianna," my father declared, nodding.

My father and mother clapped. Soon the hall was deafening. I raised our joined hands over our heads. Arianna smiled graciously as she shifted closer. I dropped her hand and encircled her waist.

Once the noise had subsided, a thin voice hollered, "Arianna Travers?"

Arianna and I shared a glance before searching the attendees. Who in my world could know Arianna's surname? Not even Jett was privy to this information.

The crowd parted, and Arianna gasped. She left my embrace and hurried toward the stairwell, kicking off her white heels as she ran. I followed, taking the steps two at a time. I trusted the woman Arianna approached. My governess, Elyse. Tears stained the older woman's face as she held open her arms.

Inspecting Elyse, Arianna slowed. She glanced over her shoulder, and I nodded, touching her arm. She closed the distance. "Mom?"

Elyse smiled brightly. "I never thought I'd see you again."

Arianna hesitated, glancing up at my parents. I nudged her toward her mother, and Arianna fell into Elyse's arms. A fountain of joyful tears followed. Warmth filled my heart, my dragon's pride flaring. Elyse's hair was once the same color as Arianna's. Although their eye color was different, I could tell they were family.

"Kyan has grown into a good man, but I can tell you stories," Elyse said, holding Arianna's face.

Arianna radiated happiness. Her eyes crinkled as she giggled. "I will hold you to it. I love learning about Kyan, and I want to know more about this place and how you found it."

"Later," Elyse glanced at me and nodded. "Today we celebrate your pairing. I could not have chosen a better man for my little girl."

I reached for Elyse's hand, bowing I kissed it. "Thank you, Elyse. I will treasure her and her love as long as I have breath."

Arianna attacked me with a hug. She grinned, her eyes watery. "You are so stinking romantic."

My heart fluttered as if it had grown wings. This beautiful woman agreed to be my mate. My dragon longed to take flight and rendezvous with Arianna alone.

"My son," the king called. "Let the ceremony proceed."

I took Arianna's small hand, then reached for Elyse's. "Please stand with us, Mother." Elyse gripped my hand as if she needed support. She nodded and walked beside me to my parents. They greeted each other with bows.

Elyse stepped back next to Jett. He linked elbows with her.

"Kyan and Arianna," my mother whispered, motioning for us to stand in front where all could see us. We faced each other with clasped hands, as we had practiced. Then my parents wove a braided thread around our wrists, the unification ritual. I held Arianna's gaze, and my heart thundered.

"Let all know and see that Kyan and Arianna are joined in unity. May their mating be blessed with happiness and many children."

The audience called blessings and well-wishes, but I only focused on my mate. I lowered my lips to hers. Her eyes fluttered closed, and her lips opened for me. I hummed and devoured her mouth with a possessiveness my dragon agreed with. She moaned, and I struggled to restrain the heat. I longed to run my fingers through her hair and touch her everywhere, but that had to wait. My dragon growled in frustration.

"You have the first dance, son," my mother said. A warm hand landed on my shoulder, and I broke the kiss. Arianna's dewy lips parted, and a soft sigh escaped.

With an adoring smile, Zaffrie handed Arianna her white heels.

I laced our fingers. We once again descended the steps. I led her to the center where the floor was tiled with Ellehcor's star and dragon crest. Arianna shifted uneasily.

"Relax, my love." I placed my other hand on her hip. The music started, and she smiled.

"It's beautiful." Arianna glanced at our parents, then swallowed. "I'm not much of a dancer. I'm afraid I'll embarrass you and your family."

"Trust me," I whispered in her ear. "We only have to dance this first dance."

She leaned her cheek against mine. "Where you lead, I will follow."

I stepped in time to the music, and after a few paces, Arianna had the rhythm. We flowed as one. My cousins and the nobles moved out of our way as we circled past.

Her golden hair glistened in the waning light like dragon

scales in the moonlight. I twirled her, her dress flaring, and I noticed a small blue dragonfly in the gathered material. A tiny remembrance of my other worldly form. I continued dancing, leading her out onto the garden terrace.

She stopped moving, her gaze fixed overhead. "The stars," she breathed. "There are so many."

I leaned against the stone wall, studying her wide silver eyes, glittering with starlight. "Just wait…"

She pressed against me, her warmth igniting my dragon. Her lips tickled my neck between words, "For… what?"

"If you keep that up you'll never know," I rumbled, my dragon close to the surface.

She stepped back, her face aglow with my inner fire. "I guess I turn you on. Literally." She giggled, then tipped my head as she met my lips. My breath caught as she swept into my mouth. Encircling her in my arms, I held her close.

"This isn't the show I paid for," Jett grumbled.

Arianna moved in my arms but didn't break the kiss.

"What does that mean?" Jett huffed, crossing his arms.

Breaking the kiss, my forehead to hers, she caressed my jaw. "Promise me we'll kiss like that every day," she whispered.

"You have my word," I vowed.

"What's that?" Arianna pointed to the sky, and I smiled.

"It's beginning." I guided her down the pathway, following the crowd. The fabric of her dress swished as she hurried.

In an open field, the spectators fanned out around three pyramids of tree trunks. Lanterns illuminated the periphery. The gathering murmured in excitement.

"Something is in the sky, blocking the stars. Are those moving black shapes dragons?" Arianna asked, her face upturned and expectant like an excited child.

"It's a Harvest Moon tradition. Three pyres are lit as the moon rises over the horizon," I pointed toward the distance, "between those columns. We recognize our ancestors who toiled in the past and appreciate the sacrifices they made to procreate the future. We acknowledge those who live now, lauding the fruits of their labor. And we bless the future, because the next generations are our hope."

"Remembering the past, honoring the present, and celebrating a hopeful tomorrow. It's a beautiful tradition." She touched my arm, then rested her head on my shoulder.

"The moon…" a woman proclaimed, and a hush fell over the onlookers.

A silver sliver crested the horizon. A trail of light illuminated the first pyre. The thumping beat of dragons' wings overhead grew louder as they drew near. "These three dragons are from an elite guardian troop who protect our borders."

They swooped low, circling the wooden pyramid. A red dragon hovered, his chest and neck glowing before he spewed fire down upon the wood. A bellow of heat rolled over us. The second dragon lit the present pyre followed by the third igniting the future tribute. The fire reached for the heavens. People mingled around the fires, drinking and dancing, but Arianna and I remained on the edge of the fray. She smiled, watching the antics of some youths, but glanced away when they kicked off their clothes to shift.

I couldn't help but chuckle as I pulled her close once more. "I'm glad you accepted my offer." Her sweet spirit would never again be downtrodden by her uncle.

"You're a wish come true. I love you, Kyan." Arianna wrapped her slender arms around my waist and kissed my chin.

Warmth filled me, unlike dragon fire. "I receive your gift of love and offer my heart forever and always."

Love a book?

Please leave a review.

Reviews are like virtual hugs for authors.

Also by Rochelle Bradley

The Fortuna, Texas Series

☆★Fortuna Full Length Novels★☆

The Double D Ranch Book
Plumb Twisted
More Than a Fantasy
Municipal Liaisons

☆★Fortuna Short Stories★☆

Here We Go Again
The Playboy's Pretend Fiancée

☆★Other Books★☆

Who's the Fairest? A Sisters Grimm Anthology

Here's your chance to find out if all Fairy Tales end in: Happily Ever After...
Or if their fates are sometimes a little bit Grimm...
Featuring authors: Andi Lawrencovna, Rochelle Bradley, Isobelle Cate, Hope Daniels & Alicia Dawn, Jennifer Daniels, SE Winters, Genevieve Gornichec, Shaunna Rodriguez, Kali Willows

Rochelle puts an artistic spin on everything she does but there are two things she fails at miserably:

1. Cooking (seriously, she can burn water)
2. Sewing (buttons immediately fall back off)

But she loves baking and makes a mean BTS (Better than Sex) cake. When in observation mode she is quiet, however, her mouth is usually open with an encouraging glass-is-half-full pun or, quite possibly, her foot.

She's a Bearcat, a Buckeye, an interior decorator, and fluent in sarcasm.

In 2008 she decided to get the stories out of her head. Midway through her first novel, hurricane Ike (yes, a hurricane in Ohio) rendered the laptop useless with a nine-day power outage. She didn't give up, but continued to pursue her dream.

Every November Rochelle takes on the challenge of National Novel Writing Month (NaNoWriMo.org) where she endeavors to write 50,000 words in thirty days. You can often hear her cheering the Dayton area Wrimos (those who join her in this crazy pursuit).

Rochelle shares her home with a big black

cat, an itty-bitty orange tiger kitty, her daughter, her son, and her Prince.

She loves to connect with readers. You can find her on Facebook (search for Author Rochelle Bradley), Twitter, Pinterest, and Instagram.

Visit Rochelle's website to sign up for her newsletter to keep up to date about future novels and book signings: RochelleBradley.com. Join the author Rochelle Bradley fan club on Facebook.